Hello!

Welcome to *Forever Phoenix*, the fourth and final book in my
Lost & Found series! Phoenix is a fiery, dramatic girl who often feels
misunderstood. When she pitches up in Millford for a fresh start after
an especially disastrous accident, it's touch and go whether she'll be
able to make a go of it . . . but once she meets cool teen band
the *Lost & Found*, everything changes. Discovering a long-lost talent
and rebuilding her shattered confidence, Phoenix finds herself
centre stage and causing a stir. Behind the scenes, she is making friends
and falling in love, but can she work out how to build bridges with her
broken family and rise from the ashes of a troubled past?

   I think you'll love Phoenix . . . and her cool sidekick, Pie! *Forever
Phoenix* is a perfect escapist read . . . warm, twisty and dramatic.
Curl up and fall into the world of the *Lost & Found*. What are you
waiting for?

Cathy Cassidy. xxx

Books by Cathy Cassidy

Lost & Found
LOVE FROM LEXIE
SAMI'S SILVER LINING
SASHA'S SECRET
FOREVER PHOENIX

The Chocolate Box Girls
CHERRY CRUSH
MARSHMALLOW SKYE
SUMMER'S DREAM
COCO CARAMEL
SWEET HONEY
FORTUNE COOKIE

LIFE IS SWEET

BITTERSWEET: SHAY'S STORY
CHOCOLATES AND FLOWERS: ALFIE'S STORY
HOPES AND DREAMS: JODIE'S STORY
MOON AND STARS: FINCH'S STORY
SNOWFLAKES AND WISHES: LAWRIE'S STORY

THE CHOCOLATE BOX SECRETS

ANGEL CAKE
BROKEN HEART CLUB
DIZZY
DRIFTWOOD
INDIGO BLUE
GINGERSNAPS
LOOKING-GLASS GIRL
LUCKY STAR
SCARLETT
SUNDAE GIRL

LETTERS TO CATHY

For younger readers

SHINE ON, DAIZY STAR
DAIZY STAR AND THE PINK GUITAR
STRIKE A POSE, DAIZY STAR
DAIZY STAR, OOH LA LA!

Cathy Cassidy

FOREVER PHOENIX

PUFFIN

PUFFIN BOOKS

UK | USA | Canada | Ireland | Australia
India | New Zealand | South Africa

Puffin Books is part of the Penguin Random House group of companies
whose addresses can be found at global.penguinrandomhouse.com.

www.penguin.co.uk
www.puffin.co.uk
www.ladybird.co.uk

First published 2020
001

Text copyright © Cathy Cassidy, 2020
Illustrations copyright © Erin Keen, 2020

The moral right of the author and illustrator has been asserted

Set in 13.55/20.06 pt Baskerville MT Std
Typeset by Jouve (UK), Milton Keynes
Printed and bound in Great Britain by Clays Ltd, Elcograf S.p.A.

A CIP catalogue record for this book is available from the British Library

HARDBACK ISBN: 978-0-241-44796-3
PAPERBACK ISBN: 978-0-241-44794-9

All correspondence to:
Puffin Books, Penguin Random House Children's
One Embassy Gardens, 8 Viaduct Gardens
London SW11 7BW

Thanks . . .

Once again, to my long-suffering partner, Liam, and my kids, Cal and Cait, for keeping the world turning while I write. Thanks to my fab friends Helen, Sheena, Jessie, Mel, Fiona, Janet, Paul, Kicki, Joan, Doreen, Aud and everyone else who has helped to keep me smiling lately. As always, I'm grateful to Carmen, Amelia, Tania, Ellen, Wendy, Mary-Jane and all at Puffin HQ, and to Erin Keen for the beautiful cover and chapter headings. Gratitude to my agent Darley and my accountant Martyn. Special shout-outs to all the cool indie bookshops and libraries out there, and most of all to YOU, my brilliant readers, for all your loyalty and support. You're awesome!

Cathy Cassidy, xxx

If you've ever been to boarding school, you'll know that you're never alone. I have a room to myself, a narrow bed right next to an old sash window that rattles in the breeze, but ten girls share this corridor. There is always, always someone around . . . except when there isn't.

School is shut for October break and I'm the only one here.

We're not allowed to light candles, but there's nobody to tell on me so I light a short stubby candle that smells of vanilla and unwrap a slice of chocolate brownie bought from the village earlier.

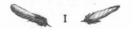

A high wind outside makes the autumn trees dance, but there's no mistaking the sharp rap on the glass. I'm on the first floor, but I'm pretty sure it's Pie, the tame magpie I rescued back in the spring, calling to see if I'm bored and in need of some company. I pull up the window and Pie flies in on a gust of wind that makes the candle flame gutter. He hops on to my shoulder.

The girls I share a dorm with think I'm trouble. Amusing trouble sometimes, but not best-friend material. Still, they're not here now so I can have my candle and my chocolate brownie, and leave the window open with the curtains fluttering. I break off some brownie for Pie and leave him scoffing it on the windowsill while I head to the communal kitchen to plunder the hot-chocolate stash.

I'm singing my heart out as I come back into my dorm room with a mug of steaming hot chocolate, but the song dies on my lips. Bright, leaping flames are racing up the curtains and black smoke is billowing from cushions stacked up on my bed beneath. There's no sign of Pie, just a few brownie crumbs on the windowsill.

I run to the shared bathroom, shove a bath towel in the sink and turn on the tap with shaking hands. Smoke fills

2

my throat as I swat at the curtains, but all that does is fan the flames and knock something off the windowsill and down into the flowerbeds below. The towel catches fire and I run back to the bathroom to get another, but when I turn the blaze has reached the corridor. Smoke blurs my eyes and fills my lungs, and I scream and scream and scream.

Magpie Rhyme

One for sorrow, two for joy

Three for a girl, four for a boy

Five for silver, six for gold,

Seven for a secret never to be told.

1

Smoke Damage

Let me get one thing straight: I did not burn down the school.

For one thing, it was clearly an accident and, for another, it wasn't actually the school, just one of the dorms. And it wasn't exactly razed to the ground – more smoke damage, really. Although the roof has gone, I admit, and quite a bit of the top floor.

Almost every single thing I owned has gone, apart from the clothes I'm standing in, but at least nobody was hurt, because of it being October half-term and everything. Pretty much everyone was at home with their families or off on flashy trips to Europe. And I raised the alarm – I

wouldn't have done that if I had been trying to burn the place down, would I? Seriously, think about it.

I am not an arsonist. I am all about saving the world, not setting it on fire, but even now the smoke has died down and the blaze is out, nobody wants to hear that. Nobody is listening.

It took two fire engines to get the fire under control in the end. I'd been trying to douse the flames myself with the hosepipe attached to the old greenhouse, but I couldn't get the water to reach high enough, and the firefighters pulled me out of the way, so after that I just watched. OK, I might have taken a couple of pictures on my iPhone, but be honest . . . wouldn't you have too?

Turns out the police thought that was highly suspicious.

I don't suppose they know many fourteen-year-old girls, because everybody I know catalogues their life in pictures. It's what we do these days.

A paramedic checks me over and tells me I'm a very lucky girl, and instead of arguing I take a deep breath and nod. No burns, no significant smoke inhalation, just a pall of toxic fumes following me wherever I go, clinging to my hair, my skin, my clothes.

'Try to get some rest,' the paramedic says. 'You're going to be fine.'

I don't bother asking where I should sleep now that my dorm room is a heap of charred and stinking rubbish. I don't tell her that I'm a million miles from fine.

The building is cordoned off and a firefighter tells me that little if anything will be worth salvaging. I feel like it's my life they're talking about.

The police swoop on me again once I've been given a clean bill of health.

'What's your name?' a weary police officer asks, and when I say it's Phoenix he frowns and asks if I'm joking. I've probably gone straight to the top of his list of possible suspects ... There I am, right in front of them, rising from the ashes. That's what a phoenix does, right?

I didn't ask to be called Phoenix, but I try my best to live up to the name, doomed forever to spring back from the ruins of whatever my last disaster happened to be. I didn't ask to be hanging around the charred remains of my former dorm at half past four in the morning either, with my slipper socks soaked by the hosepipe and great big flakes of ash in my hair.

I didn't ask to be a boarder at Bellvale Ladies College in the first place, for that matter. When you are fourteen years old and your mum is a career-obsessed control freak and your dad lives in Dubai with his new wife and kids . . . well, you don't actually have much choice about where you live.

'Was there anybody else in the building?' the police officer wants to know now. 'Were you alone when the fire started?'

'Just me,' I tell him. 'Well . . . me and Pie!'

'Pie?' the policeman barks. 'Just you and – *what*?'

I roll my eyes. 'Pie's a tame magpie,' I say. 'He was in the dorm earlier, but he scarpered long before the flames took hold. I hope he's OK!'

The policeman loses interest after that. I swear, nobody cares a bit about magpie welfare in today's society, except possibly me. He interviews me about the fire and writes lots of stuff down in a notebook, like in one of those TV detective series, but there seems to be no evidence of arson. The policeman says it is a school matter as far as he's concerned.

That's not as hopeful as it sounds – the head teacher is not my number-one fan.

8

As I turn away from the ruins, I spot something glinting in an overgrown flowerbed in the moonlight. I take a look, and there it is, the battered old Quality Street tin I keep my old diaries and secret treasures in. It was on the windowsill last night, beside the open window – *that's* what I must have accidentally knocked out into the darkness when I'd panicked, trying to put out the flames with a wet bath towel.

I've lost my laptop, my books, my clothes, my shoes, my future . . . but I have my past at least, squished into that old tin. I hold it close, not sure if I want to laugh or cry.

Eventually I am hauled into Miss Winter's office, bleary-eyed from lack of sleep and still smelling of smoke, like a kipper or a pot of badly stewed lapsang souchong tea. I'm still clutching the Quality Street tin, as if it might save me from drowning.

She frowns at me, pressing her mouth into a thin line. 'Phoenix,' she says. 'I know you and I don't always see eye to eye. I know you are going through a difficult phase right now. I know you're feeling angry –'

A difficult phase? All my attempts at holding things together dissolve into sudden fury.

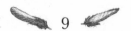

'I hate it here,' I snap. 'You know that. But I did not burn down the dorm, OK? It was an accident!'

Miss Winter's face darkens. If I didn't know better, I'd think she was angry, but somehow her ice-queen persona wins out. She is not called Miss Winter for nothing. 'Well,' she says. 'I certainly hope that it was. Your time here at Bellvale Ladies College has not been as happy as we might have wished –'

'No kidding.'

'This latest incident is most unfortunate,' she continues. 'You've made it clear that you do not want to be here. I've tried my best to be patient –'

'Have you? Can't say I noticed.'

'What's in the tin?' she asks, frowning. 'The dorm burns down and you save a tin of . . . sweets?'

That hits me right in the heart. Does she know nothing about me?

'Not sweets, memories,' I say through gritted teeth. 'You wouldn't understand!'

'I don't suppose I would,' she admits. 'I've tried my best for you, but no, I don't understand. I think, Phoenix, we have come to the end of the line.'

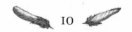

Miss Winter's long fingers fiddle with the silver necklace she always wears. It's something she does when she's particularly stressed or angry – I've seen it a lot these last few years. I can tell that she hates this as much as I do. She is not the kind of woman who likes to admit defeat. She has failed with me, though, and I can't help smiling a little at that.

'I have spoken to your grandmother,' Miss Winter says. 'She agrees with me that things at Bellvale haven't worked out. You can't go to your father in Dubai – he's said something about the timing being difficult – but your grandmother has agreed to take you. I'd ask you to pack your bags, but there won't be much to pack – and the building's cordoned off until the health and safety people have been, so don't even think about it, Phoenix.'

My shoulders slump. It's not that I had a lot to lose, but what I did have is gone, almost every last bit of it.

Miss Winter peers at her computer, clicks and prints out a couple of sheets of A4.

'I've booked you a train,' she says briskly. 'I'd drive you to the station, but I'm expecting the insurers to call, and of course there will be parents to talk to once the news of

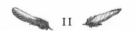

11

what's happened gets out. We can only hope the press don't get hold of it, but either way I'll need to stay here to handle things. A taxi will be here to collect you at eleven. You can pick up your tickets with this code, and there's cash in this envelope for the cab and for snacks and a taxi at the other end. It's not ideal, obviously –'

'You want me to leave right now?' I interrupt. 'Immediately? Smelling of smoke, with ash in my hair?'

'I'll find you a change of clothes,' she says grudgingly. 'You can pop into the gym to have a wash and brush-up . . .'

I blink, unable to take it all in.

'What is this?' I whisper, numb with shock. 'Have I been expelled?'

Miss Winter has the grace to look shifty. 'No need to call it that,' she says. 'That wouldn't look good for the school, and it wouldn't look good for you. Things haven't worked out – let's leave it at that. We're all agreed that this is the best solution . . .'

'Are we?' I challenge.

'Phoenix, you have left me no choice.'

The phone starts ringing on her desk, and I can see her hand reach out to take it, then pull back again. She is not going to risk speaking to insurance assessors or concerned parents until I am safely off the premises.

Well, fine.

I square my shoulders and tilt my chin and walk to the door. I pretend I am brave and tough and confident, that I am wearing platform biker boots instead of soggy slipper socks. I pretend that I am calm and cool about it all, that the sting of tears in my eyes is just a reaction to the acrid smoky stink that clings to my clothes. I pretend I don't care, and when I reach the doorway I turn and glare at Miss Winter.

'Thanks, Mum,' I say to her. 'Thanks a bunch.'

I slam the door.

My Crismas List by Phoenix Marlow age 7

1/ A tree howse

2/ Crismas sweets in a propar tin

3/ Sing on stayje

4/ Be as famuss as Ariana Grande

5/ Mum and Dad to get back together

PS I have been very good I promiss.

PPS I will be at Granny Lou's for Crismas

so dont go to wrong place.

2

Banished

Look, don't judge me. Yes, the career-mad mother I mentioned is indeed none other than Miss Winter, the steely-eyed head teacher of the boarding school that has been my prison for the last three years. Sucks, right?

You don't get to choose your parents. If you did, I clearly would not have picked a control-freak head teacher with a heart of ice and a burning ambition to rule the world.

The day I started at Bellvale Ladies College, the two of us made ground rules. We hadn't had the easiest of relationships up to that point, and we wanted to find a way to make things work. We decided the best way to do that was to ignore each other. I would tell nobody that I was related to the school's head teacher; I'd share a dorm with my classmates like everyone else.

Holidays were the only tricky bit. Dad was out of the picture – he married again a few years back and moved to Dubai. He has two marauding toddlers and a wife called Wanda who thinks I am a deranged psychopath, which is kind of awkward. Sometimes I'd holiday with a classmate, but lately I tend to hole up alone at school while Mum fusses away in the background writing school reports and polishing lacrosse trophies or whatever it is that head teachers do for fun.

Nobody ever discovered our secret. The fact that Mum changed her surname back to Winter the minute she and Dad split up helped with that, along with the fact that she has always been very good at maintaining a frosty distance. Whenever the other girls asked about my family, I acted huffy and explained that my parents cared more about work than about me. It was the truth, after all, and after a while they stopped asking.

The deal was that Mum would stay out of my life as much as possible, but if I put a foot wrong she would come down on me like a ton of bricks. No special treatment. I am surprised it took so long for the ton of bricks to fall, but fall they did, and I'm still reeling from the impact. I'm dazed and confused, but glad to be getting out of this dump, trust me.

I take a long hot shower in the gym changing rooms, washing my hair over and over with someone else's abandoned shampoo until I smell of lemons instead of bonfires.

My maniac mother delivers a change of clothes for me as promised. Unfortunately she has the fashion taste of a colour-blind OAP. There is no universe in which I would be seen dead in a yellow ruffled blouse, beige cardigan and green plaid kilt that feels like it was woven from a mixture of nettles and camel hair. I stuff the offending items into an empty locker and raid the lost property cupboard instead.

There, behind piles of boxes filled with dusty old textbooks and a wickerwork cat basket belonging to Tiger, the school cat, I find assorted items of abandoned school uniform. The pleated black skirt is pleasingly short and the grey cable-knit socks bizarrely long, and the black crew-neck sweater is so big it does the job of a coat. A pair of almost-new Ash trainers completes the look; although they're a size too big, the cable-knit socks help a little.

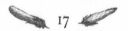

I dig about in someone's long-lost make-up bag, find a black eyeliner pencil and swipe it expertly beneath my lower lashes. My hair, still damp from the shower, falls down my back in red ringlet curls.

I trudge through the school, loitering a little outside Mum's office, scuffing the toes of my adopted trainers against the shiny wooden skirting board. Tiger the cat appears from nowhere, pressing himself against my legs and swishing his ginger tail regretfully. At least he will miss me – and Pie too, of course.

I bite my lip. Pie may or may not have been the architect of my downfall, but I cannot bear the thought of leaving him behind. Could a magpie fit into a cat basket? I run back to the gym and haul out the wicker cat basket – now all I have to do is find him. I spend the next half hour combing the grounds, calling Pie and saying a silent farewell to the place that's been home these last three years, adding a sprig of purple heather and a charred, soaked scrap of what was once my maths exercise book to the Quality Street tin as I go. It's not like I'll ever forget this place, but old habits die hard.

My magpie friend is nowhere to be seen. He's not in the tree I found him beneath back in the spring. He's not up by the summer house, our favourite hangout. He's not in the vegetable garden annoying Mr McArdle, the sour-faced school groundskeeper who's been known to take pot shots at Pie with his air rifle.

Pie is nowhere at all. He's probably flown up to the forest, upset by the smoke and the fire engines and the fuss . . . but what if he was caught in the fire after all? What if he's hurt, or worse?

'Pie, please!' I yell, but there is no answering *'chacker chacker'* call.

I can't find Pie. I can't kidnap him. I can't even wave goodbye.

As I head back to the school building, the promised taxi sweeps to a halt on the gravel drive. It's eleven o'clock exactly.

'Not much luggage then?' the driver asks, eyeing the empty cat basket and my Quality Street tin, and I can't quite trust my voice to tell him I don't have a thing in the world, at least not any more. That's when I spot Pie watching me from between the ears of one of the stone lions that perch grandly on either side of the steps, his blue-black and white plumage sleek, his bright beady eyes glinting.

'Pie!' I squeal. 'You're safe! I just knew you'd be OK!'

He spreads his wings and glides over to settle on my shoulder, making a soft, sad chittering sound. If he wasn't a magpie, I would tell him about my disgrace, my banishment. I would tell him how sad I am feeling, how he is my best friend in the world, how much I'm going to miss him. Let's face it, I'd tell him all of that anyway if only the taxi driver wasn't leaning out of the window, chewing gum and listening.

'What's that?' he asks. 'A magpie? Watch it don't peck your eyes out!'

Magpies are so misunderstood, I kid you not.

'He's a rare Caledonian long-tailed macaw,' I declare. 'His name is Pie.'

'Aye, right – and I'm Bonnie Prince Charlie,' the taxi driver says. 'Caledonian long-tailed macaw . . . pull the other one!'

I spot a pale face lurking behind the leaded glass window of Mum's office, looking sad and anxious, and for a moment I wonder if she will rush down the steps and cling on to me too, in a Pie-like display of affection. Then I realize she's on the phone, probably talking to a parent-governor about the fire and trying to pass it off as a freak lightning-strike incident.

She catches sight of me and her mouth shrinks into a pinched, pained shape, her fingers tugging at the phoenix necklace round her neck. Grandma Lou gave her the necklace on her sixteenth birthday, and apparently it inspired my name. I have a matching bracelet, a silver chain with a phoenix charm that Mum gave me when I was ten. I still wear it as a bright glimpse of times gone by. It's one of the few personal presents Mum has ever given me.

Anyway, it's clear that she isn't coming out to say goodbye. She flicks a hand in my direction in what might be a half-hearted wave – or an attempt to brush me out of her line of vision.

Pie chirrups again. Right now, he's pretty much all I have left in the world. I found him in the spring when he was a tiny fledgling, fluffy and fierce-looking with feathers sticking out everywhere. I never knew for sure if he'd fallen out of the nest or tried to fly too soon and failed, but earlier that day Mr McArdle had been boasting that he'd shot a magpie. Pie was almost certainly an orphan, so I scooped him up and put him in a cardboard box and hid him in the dorm to save him from Tiger.

I fed him cat food and hard-boiled eggs chopped into bits, and digestive biscuits soaked in orange squash – that last one wasn't actually on the list of possible foodstuffs I found on the internet, but he seemed to like it. My dorm mates weren't so keen, especially when Pie took to landing on their heads and squawking in their ears. They said magpies were bad luck, especially a lone magpie.

'One for sorrow,' the girl in the room next to mine said, quoting the old folk rhyme. I told her that was stupid, so she snitched on me, and Mum made me release Pie back into the wild.

'He's a wild creature, Phoenix,' she said. 'Not a pet!'

I knew she was right, but still I cried when I took him up the hill behind the school and let him go. I thought that would be the last I'd see of him, but Pie never forgot me. He'd swoop down on to my windowsill and tap on the dorm window with his beak, and if nobody was around, I'd sometimes let him in and we'd talk about old times together.

I am not going to leave him behind, wild creature or not. I can't.

'C'mon, Pie . . . adventure time!' I open the basket lid and watch him jump in.

He's like that – bright, brave, endlessly curious and always up for a long journey in a wickerwork basket. Well, I'm not sure about that last bit, but I'm willing to find out.

I jump into the taxi and we drive away in a hail of gravel. My life at Bellvale is over, just like that. I pride myself on maintaining a tough and confident attitude, but being turfed out without a backward glance hurts. At least I have Pie to keep me company, and that makes me feel a little less alone.

I collect my tickets, buy a sandwich and catch the train with minutes to spare. It hurtles south, taking me into uncharted territory and to a grandmother I haven't seen for four years after some family rift that Mum would never talk about. I prop my feet up on the seat opposite and try not to think about what might happen if she doesn't want me either. I have no doubt that Mum has told her I am a teen arsonist, a wild child who laughed as the school burned.

Oh, and so much for the borrowed lemon shampoo, because actually my hair still smells of dust and ashes.

*

 23

Hours later, a second cab dumps Pie and me on the pavement outside the big wrought-iron gates at Greystones. The sky explodes with early 5th November fireworks, and I can't decide whether this signals good luck for my new start or warns of explosive drama yet to come. Knowing my luck, probably the second.

I pay the cabbie and push open the gate, swinging the cat basket and clutching the Quality Street tin, trying to look cool and careless as I march along the drive. Greystones is not so much a house as a full-blown mansion, ivy-clad and slightly forbidding in the half-light.

To my left, wisps of music roll out from behind the trees, as if someone is holding an early-evening gig in the grounds of Grandma Lou's house. It's possible they are – my gran is eccentric and unpredictable. She was a famous model in the sixties – Louisa Winter, jet-setter and friend of the stars, her face on the covers of all the glossy magazines. She threw it all away a decade later, returning to Greystones with a baby bump and no sign of a husband or even a boyfriend.

The baby grew up to be my mother, Vivi Winter, a woman carved from ice and stone, a woman so unsuited to life as the daughter of a sixties wild child that you have to wonder if she was accidentally swapped at birth.

'It was no kind of childhood,' Mum once told me, sour-faced. 'Louisa was busy reinventing herself as an artist at the time – that was all she cared about. There were troops of famous people coming and going. We went on a round-the-world trip when I was seven – Europe, India, Morocco, Mozambique. Downright irresponsible. I'd rather have had a seaside holiday with donkey rides and sandcastles . . .'

'Nightmare,' I'd said. I could just imagine her as a child, dressed in sari silk and paddling in the Ganges, sulking because she wanted to be back at school, learning her three times table. In our family, the adventurous gene seems to skip a generation here and there, causing heartache and havoc all round.

My grandmother is a famous artist now – one of her paintings hangs in the Tate Britain – but Mum is no more impressed by that claim to fame than by my grandmother's famous modelling years.

She doesn't approve of Grandma Lou's house, either. Part of Greystones is a kind of hippy co-operative for assorted arty save-the-earth types. The last time I was here, there was a woman called Willow living in a yurt in the grounds who made rugs and baskets out of plaited plastic bags.

'C'mon, Pie, let's do this,' I say, but he's silent now, exhausted by the long train journey and resentful of his basket prison. I walk up the steps and ring the bell, listening to it echo ominously throughout the house. The ache in my stomach forms itself into a hard, sharp knot of dread so I tilt my chin up and fix a don't-care look on my face.

The door opens and Grandma Lou appears, a wispy creature in a paint-stained tunic and green suede clogs, her blazing auburn hair piled up haphazardly on her head and speared through with three or four paintbrushes.

I wonder if she's still angry enough with my mum over that long-ago quarrel to slam the door in my face, but her green eyes shine and she shakes her head.

'Oh, Phoenix,' she says.

That's all it takes.

A single fat and salty tear rolls slowly down one cheek as she hauls me in for a hug, and even though it's four years since I was last here, with nothing but a few Christmas and birthday presents in between, something inside me shifts and melts.

I wonder if this is what it feels like to come home.

Today Dad married Weird Wanda. She wore a white frilly dress and a tiara, like a Barbie doll come to life, only scarier.

I had to wear a discusting dress made out of oringe nylon with puff sleeves and a big collar – Wanda said it was peach satin, but it was deffinuttley oringe. I even had to wear an oringe nylon bow in my hair. Wanda told me to stop scowling because it would spoil the photograffs.

The re-sepshun was very boring with stupid speeches so I got up on the table and sang 'Here Comes the Bride', and everybody laughed except Wanda who grabbed my arm so hard as she pulled me down it left a red mark. I ate too much wedding cake and was sick all down the side of her dress, and I heard her say that I was a spiteful little attenshun seeker but it turns out I was getting ill with chicken pox so it wasn't attenshun seeking at all.

I hope Wanda gets the chicken pox too for being so mean.

I hate Wanda. Why can't I have normal parents like everybody else?

3

Free Spirit

I sit on the ancient squishy sofa as Grandma Lou drapes a crochet blanket round my shoulders and hands me a box of tissues. A tidal wave of memories surfaces – memories of the two of us making sticky paint handprints on the living-room wall, of cutting up the kitchen curtains to sew a princess dress and making a sword from corrugated cardboard to go with it, of eating banana cake at midnight, sitting on the big, low horizontal branch of our favourite oak tree. You could clamber up to it quite easily via a series of lower branches and, if I remember rightly, Grandma Lou sipped white wine out of an enamel mug while I drank Ribena.

She is not the usual kind of grandmother.

'Let it all out,' she says now, stroking my hair as the tears roll down my cheeks, an ugly, salty waterfall of pain. 'Let it go.'

So I do, and she pulls me close and I breathe in her trademark scent of strong coffee, Pears soap and turpentine. I cry a wet patch on the shoulder of her embroidered tunic dress. She tells me that things will be OK, and I want to believe her, I really do.

'Want to tell me what happened?' she asks, wiping the last of my tears and holding me at arm's length. It's something my mum never bothered to ask.

'It was my fault,' I whisper. 'But . . . I didn't do it on purpose. I lit a candle. Which isn't allowed, obviously, but it was Hallowe'en and the rest of the world was partying and dressing up and having fun, and I wanted to celebrate it, just a little bit.'

Grandma Lou nods, still stroking my hair.

'There's this tame magpie who jumps on to the windowsill all the time . . . if you leave the window open, he comes in. His name is Pie and I've known him since he was a chick – I sort of saved his life. I wanted some company, so I opened the window and in he came.'

Grandma Lou looks thoughtful. 'I see,' she says. 'A lighted candle, an open window and a marauding magpie . . . not a great combination. Does your mother know?'

I sigh. 'She can't get past the arson theory. Besides, if it turns out Pie was involved . . . well, Mum'd be even madder than she already is. She doesn't like him.'

Grandma Lou raises an eyebrow. 'Ah,' she says. 'Our little friend in the cat basket . . . that's Pie?'

'I couldn't leave him there,' I argue. 'The school groundsman shot his mother with an air rifle, and he's always threatening to get Pie too – seriously, the world sucks if you're a magpie.'

The world sucks if you are a fourteen-year-old girl with big dreams and a knack of repeatedly doing the wrong thing at any given moment too, but I don't say this to Grandma Lou.

'At least we have space for him here,' she is saying. 'Plenty of trees, a park right across the road . . .'

'Oh! I was thinking he might like to be an indoor magpie.'

'Is that fair on Pie?' she asks gently, and my hopes crumble because it isn't. I know that. Pie and I are both free spirits – and you cannot keep a free spirit in a cat basket, or not for long. I lift the basket and peer inside. Pie is in the corner, eyes beady and frightened, feathers fluffed up. He seems to be shaking, and there's been no chittering for hours now.

'No,' I admit. 'He's not an indoor bird, not any more. I'll let him go.'

'Good girl.'

I pull the crochet blanket round me and carry the cat basket to the door. It's properly dark outside now, the sky like indigo velvet. The blanket trails behind me like a cloak as I make my way down the steps and across the grass towards the ancient oak tree where my grandmother and I once ate banana cake at midnight, long, long ago.

It's the kind of tree Pie might appreciate.

I stop beneath the oak, drop to my knees and unfasten the cat-basket lid. Pie is out of there like a shot, spirits restored – he flies up on to my shoulder and hides behind my hair.

'New home, Pie,' I tell him, making my voice as upbeat as I can. 'A nice big oak, and I'm told the neighbours are friendly. There's a park close by if you want to go crazy, and no trigger-happy groundsman, I promise . . .'

Pie shows no interest in leaving my shoulder. 'I'll be right here . . . just a stone's throw away,' I whisper.

Of course, I don't know if that's true. I might end up with Dad, or maybe I'll be packed off to some other boarding school, if any can be bribed to take me. My future is hanging in the balance, but Pie doesn't need to know that.

'You'll be safe here, wherever I end up,' I tell him. 'You'll be free . . .'

I stretch an arm out to the lowest bough, and Pie hops along it and flutters into the tree. He pauses for a moment, eyes glinting, then turns and flies higher, vanishing into the dark.

I don't think I have ever felt more alone.

The night air smells of woodsmoke and autumn, and I stand for a moment breathing it in, trying to find courage for whatever the coming days will bring. My life is in tatters, but I will gather it up, stitch it together and carry on, the way I always do. I am the queen of brave faces.

As I stand in the darkness, I hear the sound of distant voices and laughter, the eerie discordant whisper of music.

Ghostly figures appear through the trees, their faces faint blurs in the darkness as they turn towards the wrought-iron gates. I shiver, the hairs prickling on the back of my neck. It's only a day after Hallowe'en, but . . . do ghosts carry guitars and violin cases?

Their footsteps crunch across the gravel as they pass through the gates and out into the night.

Grandma Lou joins me beside the oak tree. 'The Lost & Found,' she says softly.

My eyes widen. 'The . . . what?'

'Our resident teen band,' she explains. 'Although they're not actually resident, apart from Jake. They practise here in the old railway carriage, and they're fabulous. If you stay here and go to the local school, you'll meet them . . .'

I blink, register a distant blast of trumpet and echoing laughter. Surprise, disbelief and a tangle of hope and fear pulse through me.

'Stay here?' I echo.

'Seems like the best plan. Your mother says things aren't working out at Bellvale. Your father . . . well, he seems busy with his new family,' Grandma Lou says, an edge of disapproval in her voice. 'Besides, I don't think either one of them has a clue how to handle a girl like you.'

She's right about that.

'When I was your age, my parents had certain ideas of what was expected of me,' she continues. 'I didn't like those ideas. I felt misunderstood, stifled, trapped . . .'

'That's how I feel!' I exclaim.

'I know, Phoenix. You're full of spirit and mischief and wonderful, dangerous ideas . . . and your mum doesn't know how to deal with that. My parents didn't, either.'

I think of my grandmother as a teenager in the sixties, taking a train to London to make her fortune as a model. I think of her coming home again as a single mum, hanging out with pop stars and artists, travelling the world and earning fame all over again as a painter. She makes breaking the rules seem like a brave and exciting thing to do, not something to be ashamed of.

'My parents didn't mean to, but they failed me,' she says with a sigh. 'When it was my turn, and again without meaning to, I failed your mother. I was too busy following my own path to consider that Vivi might have needed something different. It's the greatest regret of my life. Perhaps it's too late to mend the rift, but I can try to make sure you're loved and safe and happy. I can look after you, Phoenix, if you want to stay.'

It looks like I'm out of options. Hanging out with my eccentric gran is all that's on offer, and to be fair it's got to be better than another term at Bellvale. Better late than never, I vow to turn over a new leaf, make Grandma Lou proud of me. No more breaking the rules, no more getting into trouble at school, no more dates with unsuitable boys. I can do it, surely?

'I'll give it a go if you will,' I whisper.

'Well then, that's sorted.' She puts an arm round my shoulder. 'Coming in?'

'In a minute,' I say, and Grandma Lou just smiles and heads into the house. I scramble up into the tree and sit astride the horizontal branch where long ago the two of us shared banana cake.

'Pie?' I call, and my black-and-white friend swoops down and on to my shoulder, chattering away.

I lean my head against the trunk and try to process the events of the last twenty-four hours, but it's all too much, so I let my mind go blank and start to sing softly, a song I made up a few months ago especially for Pie, round about the time Mum made me release him back into the wild. It's all about spreading your wings and flying high, being a free spirit.

I can't sing, I know that, but all the same I put my heart and soul into it. It's a song of sadness and a song of love, and Pie rests his head against my cheek and chitters along with me as I sing.

Diary of Phoenix Marlow, age 9

Dad and Weird Wanda are moving to Dubai. Dad says it's for work but I think Wanda wants to live as far away as possibul so I can't visit. Dad says it's very hot and I can come out for holidays, but not just yet because Wanda is having a baby. That makes me feel all sad and spikey inside.

One good thing is that I got the role of lead angel in the school Crismas play. I have to do a dance routine and sing a Crismas carol all on my own, but Mum says she proberly won't make it to the show because she's got an interview that day.

4

Bonfire

My grandmother decides to throw a Bonfire Night party. She invites everyone from Greystones as well as the ghostly teen band who practise in the old railway carriage in the grounds and assorted local friends she thinks I should meet.

Instead of making me go to school the next day, which happens to be the first day back after half-term, Grandma Lou announces I need a few days to recover from the fire and settle in at Greystones. It also gives her time to sort things out with my new school, and it's agreed that I'll start on the Friday . . . if it doesn't go well, at least I'll have the weekend to recover.

Grandma Lou marches me into the town's solitary fashion store to kit me out with the essentials – underwear, shoes, socks, a duffel coat, a couple of changes of hideously dull school uniform for Millford Park Academy, and some jeans, skirts, tops and jumpers for outside school. Everything is cheap as chips – my classmates from Bellvale College would curl their lips and sneer, but I don't care. I have clothes. I have a place to live. I have hope.

A quick dash around Superdrug completes the shopping trip, with the promise that I can borrow Grandma Lou's ancient laptop for school stuff if I need to.

As we walk up the drive towards the house, I see a man with dreadlocks and a stringy-looking rainbow-striped jumper building a bonfire just beyond the trees.

'This OK?' he calls out to Grandma Lou. 'I've cleared all the rubbish from the garage. Popping into town to collect the fireworks later . . . I'll get the low-noise kind.'

'Good work, Sheddie!' she replies. 'This is my granddaughter, Phoenix – you've met her before, I'm not sure if you remember? She's staying with me now. Phoenix, this is Sheddie. He lives in one of the apartments here. His stepson Jake is about your age.'

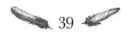 39

I can't remember Sheddie, or anyone called Jake, but then my memories of long-ago Greystones visits are sketchy at best.

'Good to see you again, Phoenix,' the man says. 'Let's hope it stays dry tomorrow night!'

I give him a half-hearted wave.

I spend the next day helping Grandma Lou to make toffee apples, blackberry crumble and pumpkin soup. This is something I've never done with Mum – she is strictly a sandwiches and ready-meal kind of mother, with a built-in disdain for seasonal celebrations. 'It's much more efficient,' she likes to say.

When the rift with Grandma Lou put a stop to Christmases at Greystones, Mum took to booking a table at a posh hotel in the village near Bellvale, because even she admits you can't have sandwiches or a ready meal on Christmas Day.

Grandma Lou is different – she rolls her sleeves up and turns on her vintage record player and laughs when I get flour on my nose.

'I'm as bad,' she says, wiping a splodge of jam from her sleeve. 'I always end up covered in flour or paint or whatever! That's something else we have in common!'

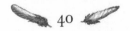

'I'm not just messy – I'm clumsy too,' I admit. 'Mum gets so cross!'

'I'm the same!' Grandma Lou says. 'Even in my modelling days, I was hopeless . . . I once fell out of a rowing boat into the River Cam doing a photo shoot for *Vogue*!'

'At least you didn't burn the school down,' I remind her, and we both grin, and that takes the sting out of the memory a little.

The whole afternoon feels like something from those feel-good family movies you sometimes get on TV, where the world becomes a better place through the power of love, kindness and home-made puddings. We're singing ancient Beatles songs as we work, and even the Ked Wilder hit, 'Phoenix', which I've always loved because of the title and because it's about a girl who has the wind in her hair and stars in her eyes. I surprise myself by remembering all the words.

'You have a lovely voice, Phoenix,' Grandma Lou says approvingly as I crash to a halt. 'So clear and strong! Have you ever thought of a musical career?'

'Nah, my voice is rubbish,' I say, suddenly self-conscious. 'Besides, Mum says only drama queens go into the music

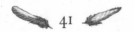

business. She wants me to train to be a neurosurgeon or something. I mean . . . deluded, much?'

'I'm not sure I see you as a neurosurgeon,' she admits. 'But I reckon you can do pretty much anything you set your mind to, Phoenix!'

'Not music, though. I got thrown out of the school choir in my first term at Bellvale . . . They said it was for talking, but I'm pretty sure it was because I can't sing!'

Grandma Lou sighs. 'Nonsense! You have an amazing voice – I've always said so.'

'Well, you're my only fan,' I say. 'Mum's never said anything, but the way she used to look at me when I was singing . . . that was enough. Like she pitied me, almost. That's when she even bothered to turn up to school plays . . .'

'Oh, Phoenix!' she says. 'If Vivi dented your confidence back then, it's because of her own anger towards me and nothing at all to do with your singing abilities. Don't let her bitterness chip away at your self-esteem!'

I laugh. I have been raised on a diet of harsh words and bitterness. My self-esteem fell to bits years ago, replaced by a brittle veneer of tough-girl carelessness. When life

throws something painful at me, I shrug my shoulders, curl my lip and look for a distraction from the hurt. The distraction might be something funny or something unexpected or shocking. Lately it's often anger, a tidal wave of it that knocks me off my feet.

'Teenage hormones,' Mum would say. She has a way of dismissing everything, putting it in a box and filing it away somewhere so she doesn't have to deal with it.

Still, I've learned that I can survive almost anything. Dad marries Weird Wanda and replaces me with two sticky-faced toddlers? No worries. Mum tells me that music is for losers and that my only talent is for rule-breaking? Too bad. Burned down the school? At least I've escaped the nightmare that was Bellvale, for now at least.

Not much can get under my skin these days, but my sweet, eccentric grandmother manages it with ease. She pulls me close, planting a toffee-flavoured kiss on my forehead before turning up the music and launching into an ear-splitting version of 'She Loves You'. The two of us sing our hearts out, dancing round the kitchen until I can't tell if the tears on my cheeks are happy ones or sad.

*

Grandma Lou's bonfire party is epic. Someone has threaded solar fairy lights through the trees, a very cool sixties-themed playlist plays out from a series of outdoor speakers, and a large folding table draped in a red-checked cloth groans under the weight of baked potatoes, pumpkin soup, toffee apples, blackberry crumble and vats of hot fruit punch.

People arrive, people of all sorts ... hippies and hipsters, a family dressed almost entirely in matching tie-dye items, little old ladies in cashmere shawls and felt hats, old blokes in *Peaky Blinders* caps and tweed jackets, a whole bunch of mismatched teenagers and gangs of unruly kids playing hide-and-seek under the trees.

Assorted people who live at Greystones come up to say hello. I vaguely remember Christmas evenings playing snakes and ladders with a couple called Laurel and Jack, and Willow the yurt lady is still there, but the others are pretty hazy ... They all seem friendly, though.

Sheddie, the bonfire-builder guy, manages the blaze and keeps the kids at a distance as the flames shoot higher. When the bonfire burns down to a warm glow, the fireworks begin ... Catherine Wheels and Shooting Stars and Traffic Lights, Fountains and Rockets, a

kaleidoscope of colour in the ink-dark sky, the smell of woodsmoke and gunpowder and sparklers sharp in my nostrils.

At one point, I spot Pie perched on the gable roof above the front door, watching the whole thing from a safe distance. He doesn't seem scared, just mildly astonished at the whole spectacle.

I am introduced to so many people I lose count of them all. There's the pink-haired librarian, the yoga teacher, the postman, the woman who works in the local supermarket and has brought along a tray of almost-out-of-date cupcakes. There's the Nigerian pastor with his wife and daughters, a Syrian refugee family, a woman in a wheelchair handing out sparklers and a very cute boy playing trumpet under the trees . . . I'm introduced to so many new people I feel like my head is spinning.

The teenagers are in that band Grandma Lou told me about, the Lost & Found. They practise in the old railway carriage behind the orchard – the one I used to pretend was a den whenever I visited as a kid. They look interesting, edgy, very different from the girls at Bellvale. They look like the kind of people I might like.

Of course, they might not like me.

'Is it true that you burned down your last school?' a fierce girl with green dip-dyed hair and purple earmuffs asks me as I hand out mugs of pumpkin soup.

'My, my – news travels fast out in the sticks,' I quip.

'Says the girl who just arrived from the wild Scottish countryside,' she counters, pulling down the earmuffs to hear me better. 'It's something I overheard . . . I won't tell anyone. Is it true?'

'Not exactly,' I admit. 'It was only one dorm.'

'Interesting,' she says. 'I'm Bex . . . bass player with the Lost & Found. And you're Phoenix . . . which is appropriate, really. Rising from the ashes and all that.'

'Arson has always been my life's ambition,' I say with a shrug. 'What can I say? I'm a twisted fire-starter.'

Bex narrows her eyes. 'If you say so. Louisa Winter always does things in style, but a bonfire party to welcome you to Millford is a stroke of pure genius.'

'Hopefully they won't burn me at the stake come midnight . . .'

'Hopefully not. They're sending you to Millford Academy, right?'

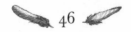

'Yes – tomorrow.'

'Place is a dump,' Bex says. 'Roof leaks, never enough books, head teacher from the time of the dinosaurs . . . but most of the teachers are OK when you get used to them. You'll be fine. If you have any trouble, give me a shout.'

She stalks away with her mug of soup and I'm left blinking.

'Phoenix! Phoenix, come over here!' Grandma Lou is waving from the darkness, and I abandon the pumpkin soup and head in her direction.

Her eyes are bright beneath a green tam-o'-shanter hat and she has an ancient embroidered shawl wrapped round her shoulders. It's cold now, and without the fireworks the sky is velvet dark, sprinkled with tiny stars.

'I want you to meet Marley Hayes,' she says, and I turn to smile at a cute teenage boy shivering in a vintage jacket and punk band T-shirt. I know the type . . . he'd rather freeze to death than put on a jumper and a beanie hat.

'Hey, Phoenix,' he says, grinning.

I smile politely, unimpressed.

'Marley here is one of the founders of the Lost & Found,' Grandma Lou explains. 'You've met some of the band

already – but Marley's been telling me that the band have lost their lead singer. Such a shame, and right when they're on the brink of breaking through!'

'Sasha's had to step down,' Marley says, nodding across at a pretty blonde girl writing her name in the air with a sparkler while the sandy-haired boy at her side looks on. 'Personal reasons. So we'll be auditioning . . . We need someone good and we need someone fast. Plus, y'know, someone who looks the part. Has stage presence. We were about to release our first single, and we'd been in talks with a national TV show . . .'

In your dreams, I think, listening to Marley's spiel. This boy is living in a fantasy world . . . but one that my grandmother seems to buy into, somehow.

'I was telling Marley about you!' Grandma Lou rushes on. 'Amazing voice, natural performer, bags of confidence . . . why not audition, Phoenix? I'm a great believer in fate!'

I don't know where it comes from, but shock and shame and anger flood through me like a tidal wave.

I cannot sing. I got thrown out of the school choir. My mother has never had a single word of praise for my singing, Weird Wanda says I am an attention-seeking menace, and I can't help wondering if even Grandma Lou may have been laughing at me behind my back as we sang sixties tunes yesterday. Audition for a band? Not in a million years, even if it is just a poxy teen band from some middle-of-nowhere small town. No way.

'Come along to the old railway carriage on Saturday at midday and we'll see what you've got to offer,' Marley Hayes is saying, like he's doing me a favour. 'Don't be daunted by our success . . . we'd be glad to give you a listen.'

I try my very hardest to hang on to my temper, really I do, but it's a losing battle.

'You'll give me a listen?' I echo. 'That's good of you. As for your so-called success . . . I've never heard of you before, and I don't suppose I ever will again. Thing is, Marley, I'm not interested in singing, I'm not interested in music, and I'm not interested in your cruddy little band. Not. Interested. Got it?'

Marley's eyes narrow. 'No worries, I've got it,' he flings back. 'We were looking for a lead singer, anyhow, not a drama queen! Sorry, Louisa . . . it was kind of you to introduce us, but we really don't need abuse from arrogant, ill-informed strangers!'

Arrogant? Ill-informed? Drama queen? Rage boils up inside me.

I turn on my heel, shove through the crowd and march up the driveway with fists clenched. I'm angry with Grandma Lou too – I thought she was different, that she understood me. But she doesn't, and now that she knows I have a foul temper on top of my fire-starter tendencies she'll probably pack me off back to Mum without a second thought. It may have taken me a few days, but I've messed up again. I am a walking, talking disaster zone.

I stomp up the steps and into the house, slamming the front door hard.

Diary of Phoenix Marlow, age 9½

I have not written anything for a few weeks as there has been a lot happening. Mum got a new job as deputy headmistress of a posh bording school in Scotland, and we have moved to a village but I can't spell the name of it. It rains a lot and everyone says it snows in winter.

   I have started at the local school and everyone thinks my aksent is funny but that's OK cos I think the same about them. I am settling in and Miss McCarey wants me to do a solo in a singing competishun. Mum says I mustn't let it go to my head cos they're probably only trying to be kind. I wish Mum would be kind sometimes.

5

New Girl

I'm still sulking majorly about the whole audition stitch-up the next day. I shower and dress in my new budget black uniform and stomp downstairs to face my fate, but Grandma Lou is oblivious to my mood, humming merrily as she makes porridge.

'Honey or apricot jam on your oatmeal?' she asks brightly, and instead of yelling that she can keep her stupid breakfast I bite my lip and ask for jam. It's what I always used to have when I was little and visiting.

'Sweeten you up a bit,' she says, and I glance at her sharply but she's smiling, setting jam and Greek yoghurt on the table. 'Big day ahead.'

I take a deep breath in. 'Last night,' I say. 'When you were teasing me about auditioning for that stupid band . . .'

'Teasing you?' she echoes. 'I wasn't teasing. I think you should give it a go! Although Marley has a temper to match yours, so you might have some bridges to build.'

'Like that's ever gonna happen,' I say. 'He's an idiot, and I can't sing!'

Grandma Lou just laughs. 'He certainly didn't hold back, but I don't blame him when you were the first to attack,' she says. 'As for the singing – well, Vivi really has done a job on you, hasn't she? Of course you can sing. You have a huge natural talent for it. Vivi doesn't like it much because she doesn't have that talent herself, and also because it reminds her of her father. It's very unfair of her to take all that out on you.'

'Her father?' I say, but Grandma Lou is scribbling something in her sketchbook and seems not to hear. 'What about her father?' I push, because according to Mum the identity of my grandad has always been a well-kept secret. I'd like to know more – who wouldn't? – but it's no use. My grandmother has zoned out.

'I have an idea for a new painting,' she tells me with a wink. 'I want to get it planned out now while it's fresh in my mind. There's cash on the counter for your lunch – have a good day, and if that temper of yours creeps up on you, count to ten and remember that it's this or boarding school again. I really don't think either of us want that, do we?'

'No,' I admit. 'We don't.'

I finish my porridge, pocket the lunch money and set off for Millford Park Academy. Grandma Lou took me in two days ago to meet the head, a nervous man called Mr Simpson with the permanently disappointed look of someone who thinks he's wasted on a small-town secondary. Seriously, he should go and work with Mum. He'd look even more washed up and miserable in a tweed suit.

It's easy enough to follow the crowds of kids mooching along with backpacks and blazers. After three years at boarding school, I have no clue if I'll be able to fit in here, but I'll give it my best shot.

I march in like I own the place, chin high, skirt swishing, an expression of bored disdain on my face to camouflage the fear that churns inside me.

If anyone finds out I've just come from boarding school, I'll be open to a whole lot of teasing; if anyone finds out about the fire, I'll be expelled before I've even started. My safest bet is to keep a low profile and give my best mystery-girl impression.

Then I remember that the green-haired girl from last night's party already knows my darkest secret and has probably spread it all round the school by now. I am doomed.

'Phoenix!' a familiar voice calls, and there lounging against a doorway is Bex, she of the dip-dyed green hair, the girl with the power to destroy my school career before it has even begun. Unless I can stop her spreading the word on my dodgy past, that is.

'Hey,' I reply, careful to stay cool. 'This is it then?'

'It is,' Bex says. 'Not planning anything yet, are you? If there's going to be a fire alarm, can you save it until the afternoon, because I have a timed essay in English and I'd quite like to get it over with!'

'Maybe,' I reply. 'Out of interest, where did you hear about the fire? It's not the kind of thing my gran would go telling people . . .'

Bex shrugs. 'She didn't, exactly. I'd left my phone at the old railway carriage and I legged it over next morning to fetch it. Louisa was gardening – planting snowdrops and tulips, she said. I found my phone, and when I went past I heard her on her mobile, talking to your school, I think. She said something about a fire and she sounded quite angry and upset, so . . . well, I'm not proud of it, but I hid behind some trees so as not to walk right into it and embarrass her. For what it's worth, she was quite certain that you'd been wrongly accused, and she insisted the school send you to her.'

I stifle a smile. Good old Grandma Lou.

'Jake told us Louisa's granddaughter had moved in . . . I guess I put two and two together.'

'Right,' I say. 'Just don't tell the world, OK? I'm in enough trouble without getting chucked out of another school, and I'd quite like to stay with my gran for a while . . .'

'I'm no gossip,' Bex argues. 'I've been in enough trouble myself in the past to go stirring things up for someone else. I haven't even told Lexie what I overheard, and she's my foster sister.'

'OK,' I concede. 'Thanks.'

Anything else I might have said is drowned out by the school bell, an especially loud and piercing alarm that signals the start of lessons. The corridor is a sea of bodies, pushing, shoving and elbowing their way to class.

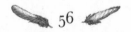

56

'Where are you supposed to be?' Bex asks above the racket.

'Registration in room 53, wherever that is – class 9B . . .'

'I'll show you,' she says, stepping into the scrum. I am astonished to see the crowd part for her, and I follow her through a rabbit warren of corridors and stairs until we reach room 53.

'You might come across some of the band, depending on your timetable,' Bex is saying. 'Failing that, we'll catch you at lunchtime. We sit at the back of the canteen on the right-hand side. I know Marley wants to ask you to audition –'

'He already did – I said no,' I snap. 'It's a sore point.'

'Gotcha,' Bex says. 'Too bad. Anyhow . . . see you later!'

She strides away along the now-empty corridor, and I take a deep breath, knock on the door and walk inside to face my fate.

In the end, it's not so bad. I manage to survive registration, French, maths and art. I do not set the school on fire, I do not reveal my delinquent past, and I do not get expelled. Instead I get lots of homework, some unwanted attention from nosy girls and flirty boys, and a little bit of praise from my new art teacher who thinks I have potential. Who knew?

At any rate, I manage the work in maths and French OK, and when we change classes I am almost sure I spot the cute boy from last night's party, the one who was playing trumpet in the trees. Bonus, right?

At lunchtime I find the canteen and queue for a hot lunch, which looks a lot better than the gruel I had to put up with at Bellvale. I'm steering through the crowd, balancing my tray and trying not to spill my orange juice, when something or someone kicks my ankle. I trip, and the whole tray goes flying – crockery smashes, food spatters everywhere, and I'm on my hands and knees in a puddle of orange juice as a roar of applause ripples round the canteen.

It's not quite the impression I was hoping to make.

'Clumsy, aren't you, new girl?' a cold voice says, and I look up to see a mean-faced kid with bleach-blonde hair sneering down at me.

'You're out of order, Sharleen,' the boy beside her says – the cute trumpet boy from last night's party again. 'It's her first day!'

'Shut it, Lee,' she hisses, jabbing him with an elbow so he almost loses his grip on his own tray of food.

I'm on my feet now, pushing soggy tendrils of hair back from my face. My eyes meet Sharleen's cold, flinty ones and the penny drops.

'You tripped me,' I say. 'You don't even know me, but you tripped me over on my first day. Wow . . . just wow. Why would you do that?'

Sharleen laughs. 'I didn't touch you, new girl,' she snaps. 'You weren't looking where you were going. I'll give you some advice for free, though – watch your back. And don't tread on my toes again. OK?'

She struts away, and I have the strongest urge to grab her bleach-blonde ponytail and yank her right back, yell in her face and shove her backwards across the nearest table of Year Sevens. My arm shoots out to do exactly that, but a firm hand grabs my wrist and pulls me back.

'Don't,' Bex says into my ear. 'She's not worth it!'

The cute boy is on his knees helping a weary dinner lady clean up the mess of my fall, and a girl I remember vaguely from last night's party appears with a fresh tray of food while another offers a clean tissue to help me wipe myself down.

'I'm Lexie,' the girl with the food tray tells me. 'This is Happi, and that's Lee doing the clean-up job. You know Bex already, I think?'

'Yeah . . . yeah, I do. What even happened there?'

'You met Sharleen Scott, Millford Park's snarkiest bully,' Lexie says with a sigh. 'At a guess, I'd say she didn't like the look of you. Waist-length auburn curls, big green eyes, short skirt . . . she reckons you're a threat. Plus, you're new and alone, so she has you pegged as vulnerable.'

'Does she now?' I say.

'Obviously she got that wrong,' Bex cuts in. 'But Sharleen has never been the brightest crayon in the box. She also has the attention span of a goldfish, so try to forget it . . . she most probably will. Seriously.'

'Come and sit with us,' Lexie grins. 'Show Sharleen you've got a whole bunch of friends already!'

I allow myself to be led across to the corner table where the Lost & Found are sitting, but I won't forget Sharleen Scott, I know.

I don't think I'll forgive her, either.

Diary of Phoenix Marlow, age 11

My first day at Bellvale Ladies College was horrible.
The girls look down on me because I haven't been to prep
school, just the local primary. They keep asking about
my parents but Mum has been promoted and is the new
headmistress here and nobody can ever know that or my
life is over. Mum agrees because she doesn't want anyone
to think there's any favouritism going on, or maybe because
she is ashamed of me, who knows.

Anyway, I kept quiet, and in the dinner hall one
girl asked what the big deal was and said maybe my
parents were in prison for murder or something, so I
pulled her plaits and threw my chocolate milk all over
her ugly bottle-green blazer. I got a week's worth of
detention and litter picking for my trouble. Favouritism?
Don't make me laugh.

I will never get used to this place.

I hate, hate, hate it.

6

Fame at Last

'We're adopting Phoenix,' Bex announces to the kids on the corner table. 'For her own safety. She seems to have made an enemy of Sharleen Scott, which clearly makes her one of our own.'

Marley Hayes, the gobby kid I scrapped with at last night's party, looks up and sneers. 'You've got rice pudding in your hair,' he says, and I scowl at him and dab again with one of Lexie's tissues.

'Take no notice, he's horrible to everyone,' Lee remarks. 'Sit down. Chill.'

I take a closer look at Lee ... I clocked him last night, a cute boy playing trumpet under the trees, but close up he's more interesting-looking than conventionally handsome. His mouse-brown hair is jaw-length and wavy, hanging in curtains around a narrow face with killer cheekbones and a lopsided smile. He winks at me, and I sink on to a chair with relief. A sea of faces, mostly familiar from last night's party, grin across at me.

'It's a rite of passage here to fall foul of Sharleen,' says Sasha, the blonde girl who used to be the band's lead singer. 'Trust me, we've all been there.'

'She hates anyone she reckons might be a threat,' Happi agrees. 'Prettier, cleverer, cooler . . . she must be massively insecure.'

'Or massively spiteful,' a quiet, serious-looking boy with hipster specs chips in.

'Or that,' Lexie concedes, and whips the tissue from my hands to finish the clean-up job. 'There . . . you're good as new.'

'Thanks,' I say. 'Not sure what I did to hack her off.'

'Most likely it was just your naturally sweet and gentle nature,' Marley says, laying on the sarcasm with a trowel. 'I expect you make friends wherever you go –'

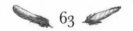 63

'Children, children,' Bex interrupts. 'Drop it, Marley, OK? The two of you got off on the wrong foot last night, but Phoenix is new here . . . Play nice!'

Marley raises one eyebrow. 'Whatever,' he says. 'I can play nice if you can . . .'

I shrug. 'I'll give it a go . . .'

'So yeah,' Bex is saying. 'We're the Lost & Found. You've met Marley, our self-styled leader. He plays guitar and he's not as much of a loser as he might seem . . .'

'Aww, Bex, you're too kind,' Marley quips.

As well as Bex, Marley, Sasha, Lee, Lexie, Happi and the boy with the hipster specs, I notice a younger boy, drumming on the tabletop with his cutlery, who almost certainly has to be Marley's brother. There's a striking, curvy brunette who I'm sure was helping with the sparklers last night, and Lexie is snuggling up to a handsome, sad-eyed boy with bird's-nest hair who is doodling in a mini sketchbook – I recognize him from the Syrian family I met last night.

'Marley's brother Dylan is our drummer,' Bex continues. 'George plays cello in the band, Sasha was our lead singer until very recently, and Jake, our tech guy, you already know from Greystones. Lee plays trumpet and generally causes havoc wherever he goes, Happi and Romy are our violinists, Lexie does backing vocals and lyrics, and Sami plays flute. He's from Syria, which is kind of awesome. That's everyone, I think!'

I manage a smile in between mouthfuls of veggie shepherd's pie. 'It's good to meet you all! I'm Phoenix, and you probably all know I'm staying with my gran for a bit. I had no clue until a few days ago that she had a rock band hiding out in her back garden . . . That's pretty cool. Why are you called the Lost & Found?'

'We were all a bit lost . . . and then we found each other,' Lexie says, and my eyes widen at her openness. After a lifetime of trying to hide my feelings, it's kind of refreshing.

'We were all set to release our first EP and video,' Bex says. 'We were recording down in Devon with Ked Wilder . . .'

I blink again. It looks like Marley's spiel about the band last night wasn't so far off the mark after all. 'Ked Wilder the sixties pop legend?' I check. 'Sang that old song "Phoenix"? For real? I think my gran knew him, back in the day!'

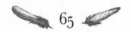

'That's the one, and yes, they're still good friends,' Lexie tells me. 'Louisa told him all about us, and we spent half-term at his recording studios in Devon. It was amazing! We came so close . . .'

'What happened?'

'I got ill,' Sasha explains. 'Absence seizures. It's a kind of epilepsy. And I wasn't enjoying the limelight anyway. I'm more of a behind-the-scenes girl. I feel bad, dropping everyone in it . . .'

'Don't, Sash,' Marley says sadly. 'You have to do what's best for you. We'll manage – we're auditioning from midday tomorrow at the old railway carriage. Who knows, there might even be someone as good as you out there!'

'Any contenders?' I ask, trying to build one of those bridges Grandma Lou mentioned earlier.

'Not really,' Lexie replies. 'A few locals, some unknowns coming over from Birmingham. Even Sharleen Scott applied, believe it or not. As if . . . you've seen what she's like . . . We can't just take anyone – it has to be the right person.'

'Someone with a brilliant voice, bags of confidence and a really strong look,' Marley says, giving me the side-eye.

'We can even overlook a snarky temper for the right person . . .'

'No,' I say, putting down my fork. 'If you're talking to me, Marley Hayes, then no. Is this a set-up?'

'Definitely not,' Bex promises. 'Marley's a chancer!'

'I'd audition the school janitor if I thought it'd help the band,' he says with a shrug. 'This is an emergency – we can't hang around or we'll miss our moment. You can't blame me for trying!'

'I told you last night,' I argue. 'I can't sing!'

'Oh?' Sasha says with a frown. 'That's not what Jake reckons . . .'

I look at Jake, and watch two spots of pink bloom on his cheeks. He's Sheddie's stepson, the boy who lives in the basement flat at Greystones.

'I was heading home the other night and I heard you singing,' he says. 'You were sitting in the oak tree, and it was dark and it seemed kind of a private moment, but it was hard not to hear all the same. You sounded . . . well, incredible. Awesome . . .'

When you've been to boarding school, you get used to having little or no privacy, but I'm still mildly hacked off

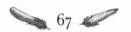

that Jake wandered past the other night when I was singing to Pie. I'm also shocked to hear him describe my singing voice as incredible and awesome.

'I just happened to mention it to Marley,' Jake is saying.

'And I mentioned it to Louisa,' Marley adds. 'She said you had a great voice and she's right about most things, but don't worry – I get the message. No go. You can't blame me for trying!'

'Guess not,' I admit.

'I have a meeting tonight with some bigshot guy from the council, too, about a really exciting gig opportunity,' Marley says. 'Could be a big break for us!'

'The timing is wrong,' Bex points out. 'You can't book us for anything right now, Marley, not until we get a new lead singer!'

'Obviously. I know that!'

'We don't need another "big break" moment – we need a singer,' Lexie agrees.

'Wish I hadn't mentioned it now!' Marley growls. 'I was thinking out loud, that's all. And, Phoenix, no hard feelings if the muso life is not for you. I guess we sort of hoped you were the answer to our prayers . . .'

'I'm more like your worst nightmare,' I mutter.

'I quite like nightmares,' Marley says.

I trudge home through a steady drizzle that soaks my cheap blazer and turns my hair to frizz, but, as I get to the edge of the park, Pie flies over and makes a clumsy landing on my shoulder. He rides all the way back to Greystones chittering into my ear. I think he has forgiven me for kidnapping him.

Back at the house Grandma Lou has freshly baked ginger biscuits waiting, and a hug for me the moment I step through the door.

'Good day?' she asks, and I smile and let my encounter with Sharleen Scott slide away.

'Yeah, really good,' I say with a grin.

'I'm glad!' she tells me. 'Me too . . . I've been drawing outside, getting to know your little friend! Take a look!'

Grandma Lou's studio is covered in big charcoal sketches of Pie. There he is with wings outstretched, with his head arched back, sitting on a tree branch, strutting across the grass. There he is in all his splendour, a cheeky, flint-eyed creature, beautiful and brash.

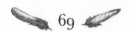

'They're amazing! Are you going to paint him?' I ask, remembering Grandma Lou's distinctive paintings of timeless, stylized humans alongside mysterious animals. 'Are you putting Pie in a picture?'

'I hope so,' she says. 'I'm still working on ideas, but I have something in mind. I'd like to do some sketches of you too. Will you sit for me after tea?'

'Sure,' I say. 'I do have English homework . . . nothing much, only a piece of creative writing on the theme of fireworks. I mean, original, much?'

'Make it original,' Grandma Lou says. 'You can make it anything you want it to be.'

I like this take on things – it's the polar opposite of Mum's view, which is that everything should be done by the book. In her eyes, a poem about fireworks should rhyme and be stuffed with metaphors, similes and at least one iambic pentameter in every verse. (No, I don't know what one is, either.) The anything-you-want-it-to-be approach is way more appealing.

After tea, we curl up on the squashy sofas in the living room, me with a new notebook and pen, Grandma Lou with a sketchbook and pastels. I try to pretend that she isn't drawing me, but after a while I forget and zone it out. There's an upbeat sixties LP on the old-fashioned record player and the stove is lit, an ancient enamel coffee pot on top . . . the room smells of woodsmoke and coffee.

I think back to last night's fireworks display, then remember Grandma Lou's words. When I touch my pen to paper something unexpected comes out. It takes an hour of scribbling, scoring out, searching for the right words, but at last I have a poem, and it's not the one I planned to write at all.

FIREWORKS

She looks no different to you or me,
There's an anger there you just can't see.
You don't know a thing about what's in her heart,
You don't know about a life torn apart,
Or how it lights a fire inside,
Fuelled by hurt and loss and pride.

Chorus: Light blue touchpaper, stand well back.
          This girl's on fire, your worst nightmare.
          You'd better handle with care.

Sometimes she's happy, sometimes she's sad,
Sometimes she's good and sometimes she's bad,
Sometimes she thinks things will work out fine,
And then they don't, time after time.
There's a lot of good in her messed-up heart
But things were stacked against her from the start.

Chorus

A girl like her can never come good,
Fire and anger are in her blood
But sometimes you need to light a spark.
It's better than sitting alone in the dark,
Just don't fan the flames or stoke the fire
And stand well back as the flames burn higher.

Chorus

7

Sing

The next morning, I wake up with a weird, fizzing, hopeful feeling inside me. I'm singing in the shower, turning the 'Fireworks' poem into a song with a melody borrowed from one of those old sixties tunes Grandma Lou likes to play. The result is fast and fierce and surprisingly upbeat, and as long as I keep the shower running there is no danger of anyone else hearing and laughing at me.

Grandma Lou is in her studio already, mapping out painting ideas on huge rolls of sugar paper with charcoal and chalk, so I help myself to toast and head outside, huddled in my new black duffel coat, woolly scarf and fingerless gloves.

As I climb the big old oak and settle myself on the horizontal branch with my back against the trunk, Pie drifts down and lands on my shoulder.

'Hey,' I say softly. 'Can you tell fortunes? One for sorrow, two for joy?'

Pie gives two short cries, which I translate to mean joy. 'School was OK,' I tell him. 'Apart from this horrible girl called Sharleen who tripped me up in the lunch hall. I mean, psycho or what? I was very restrained, though. I didn't fight back . . .'

Pie snuggles in, ruffling his wings in sympathy.

'I met the band properly, and they're OK. Even Marley, although he's a bit full of himself. I got asked again to audition – they think I actually can sing, which is clearly not true, so I'd be wasting their time. And only drama queens go into the music business, anyway . . .'

Pie gives a loud, raucous caw, as if suggesting that he might audition himself. He'd be OK . . . he definitely likes the limelight.

'Maybe it'd be fun,' I consider. 'To be in a band. In an alternate universe, I mean, one where I can sing and don't let people down the whole time. I could be famous . . . the

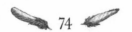

next big thing. Mum'll see me singing on TV and realize how wrong she was!'

It worries me slightly just how much I like the idea of showing Mum that I am not a total waste of space, that I can shine at something after all. I've waited my whole life for her to see something good in me.

'It probably won't be music, though,' I tell Pie. 'Or poetry, come to that . . .'

I take my notebook out of my pocket and sing him the 'Fireworks' poem with its newly added sixties melody. I have a good look around first, because after all you never know who might be walking past beneath, but everything is quiet and Pie seems to like the song. This is probably the closest I'll get to a career in music, but as always it lifts my spirits and puts a smile on my face. After a while, the sound of guitar, violin and drums drifts towards me as the Lost & Found warm up for the auditions, and at midday the first hopeful strides in through the wrought-iron gates, looking nervous and slightly lost. I decide to keep a tally in my notebook.

1. Male, 17 or 18, longish hair, mirrored sunshades . . . in November? In there no more than 10 mins, not a good sign.

2. Male, looks like the kid from the Home Alone movies, maybe ten years old if that. Chance of success, zero.

3. Female, ancient ... is she someone's mum? Not a chance.

4. Male, 15ish. Spiked-up hair that looks like it's been fixed in place with superglue. Audition lasted 15 minutes.

5. Female, very pretty, came out crying. Not looking hopeful.

6. Sharleen Scott - she isn't even meant to be auditioning! After two minutes she came out swearing then sat under my tree smoking a cigarette and wiping her eyes angrily. She didn't see me, as there is still a good covering of goldy-brown leaves. Felt a bit sorry for her but also kind of wished Pie might choose this moment to do something unspeakable on her head. He didn't.

And that's that ... she is the last, and it's still only half one. I slide down from my branch with Pie fluttering nearby until I'm safely grounded again. In spite of the duffel coat and fingerless gloves, I'm half frozen and my mind is on a hot drink, a warm fire and maybe something cheesy and feel-good on Netflix.

As I kick my way through the fallen leaves, the Lost & Found appear through the trees.

'I did warn him,' Bex says, before I can open my mouth. 'We've all warned him. He won't listen!'

'Phoenix, I'm just asking you to give us a chance,' Marley argues. 'No, actually, I'm begging you! Bribing you, even. We have hot chocolate back at the old railway carriage. Biscuits too!'

'Why not come and chill for a bit?' Lee says, looking rakish today in a battered trilby hat with a feather in it. 'We can hang out . . .'

'And you can sing,' Marley says.

'Or not,' Lexie adds, rolling her eyes as she beckons them back to the old railway carriage. 'Singing is optional. But we really do have biscuits, promise! Is that a tame magpie? Cool!'

'His name is Pie,' I say. 'I raised him from a chick, kind of.'

'Don't suppose he can sing, can he?' Marley says, huffing, and Pie stands tall and treats him to an

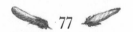

ear-splitting '*crrraaaaw*' screech, which goes to prove that he is an excellent judge of character.

'Great, even the magpie hates me,' Marley grumbles. 'Think I'm better off digging myself a hole in the ground to hibernate for the winter like Mary Shelley.'

'Hey,' Lexie says. 'She's in a box in the garage, not a hole in the ground . . .'

'She's a tortoise,' Lee tells me, grinning. 'In case you were wondering.'

'I was, a bit . . .'

'All I'm saying is that Mary has the right idea,' Marley mutters. 'I want the whole thing to go away. Seriously, I can't face another round of no-hope auditions like that last lot. And we were so *close*! The idea of starting all over again is gutting!'

'It's my fault,' Sasha says quietly. 'I've ruined everything. I'm so, so sorry!'

'It's not your fault at all,' Lexie states. 'You were brilliant, Sash, but from what you told us you haven't been happy since the start. You did the right thing to step out of the lead. Absolutely none of this is your fault!'

Sasha doesn't seem convinced.

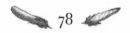

'We were close, like Marley says, but not close enough,' Bex points out. 'No good getting all worked up over what might have been. We have to find a new singer and carry on!'

'How, though? It's driving me nuts!' Marley says.

Everyone piles into the old railway carriage, and Pie doesn't miss a beat as I follow them in. He can definitely be an indoor magpie when he wants to.

I blink at the transformation. The cold, dusty sixties time-capsule den where I spent endless childhood hours drawing maps of imaginary kingdoms and dressing up in Grandma Lou's collection of weird vintage dresses is gone, replaced by brightly painted floors and woodwork in rainbow colours, bench seats upholstered in tulip red and sky-blue velvet. A little wood burner ensures the place is toasty warm, and I shrug off my duffel coat and perch on an old-fashioned armchair, while Pie hops up and down along the back of it.

A drum kit takes pride of place in the middle of the carriage, and Dylan sits behind it, automatically beginning a gentle backbeat. Happi switches on an electric kettle, grabs a jar of instant hot chocolate from the cupboard and passes round a tin of the promised biscuits while the others slump a little, picking at their instruments half-heartedly.

'Was there really nobody suitable?' I ask politely. 'At the auditions?'

'No. I mean, they weren't all totally awful, but they were wrong for us,' Lexie explains. 'Still, we'll find someone!'

'That's the point – it can't be just anyone,' Marley says with a scowl. 'We have a sound, a style – we need the right person. Someone who fits, someone who gets what we're trying to do . . .'

'It's not me,' I tell him gently.

'You've made that clear,' he says. 'Let's face it, this is an impossible task. We advertised the auditions in Millford and Birmingham, but that's not enough. We've been clutching at straws. The person we need could be in Croydon or Cardiff or Kathmandu! This whole thing is hopeless. Sorry, you lot . . . I think this is the end of the line for the Lost & Found. I'm done. Over and out.' He slumps down on the bench beside me, looking broken.

Lee throws a cushion at Marley's head and tells him not to be a quitter, and the others chime in their agreement.

They seem genuinely upset at the idea that he might leave the band, and I notice that Lexie is fighting back tears as she hands me the promised hot chocolate. It's all getting a little heavy.

'Is this yours, Phoenix?' Romy asks, picking up something from the floor. 'Think it might have dropped out of your coat pocket. Oh . . . d'you write songs?'

I make a grab for the notebook, but Marley is faster. He snaps out of his gloom, jumps up and swipes it from Romy's hand, scanning the open page with interest. A slow smile lights up his face.

'They're not songs,' I argue. 'More . . . poems, maybe. The "Fireworks" one is English homework . . .'

'It's a song lyric,' Marley tells me. 'Obviously it is. Got a melody yet?'

'Not really,' I say. 'I don't know anything about that kind of thing. I just write stuff sometimes . . .'

'I'd say it's a song lyric, too,' Bex says, raising an eyebrow at the notebook. 'Look, couldn't you audition briefly, so we can cross you off the list?'

'I'm not even on the list!'

'Of course you are,' Marley says. 'You're our only chance!'

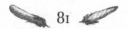

'Because Jake overheard me singing in a tree?' I scoff. 'That's crazy! You can't take his word for it!'

'We didn't,' Marley says with a shrug. 'He recorded you on his phone so we could all listen.'

Jake has the grace to look guilty. 'You weren't supposed to tell her that . . .'

I'm almost speechless – but not quite. 'You've been spying on me!' I protest. 'Sneaking round, recording me in the dark! Unreal!'

'The point is, you've got an amazing voice,' Bex cuts in. 'We've heard it. Go on, Phoenix – give it a try!'

'You're meant to be on my side!' I say to Bex.

'I sort of am,' she says. 'But I'm on the band's side too. Why can't it be the same side?'

'It can't,' I snap. 'Singing when you're on your own is not the same as singing in public. OK, so I like singing. It doesn't mean I'm any good at it. And I can't sing in front of people . . .' I say.

'Can't or won't?' Marley taunts. 'C'mon – we're desperate! This is an emergency, and all we're asking is for is one tiny audition, three minutes of your time. Jake, can you play that rough cut of "Watch Me Disappear", so Phoenix can get a feel for what we do?'

Jake slots a smartphone into a small speaker unit and presses play. I sip my hot chocolate as a sad, soulful song unfurls, and, although this song is not really my style, the tiniest shiver slides down my spine at the sound of it. Marley is right – the Lost & Found do have something. There's an energy, a rawness in their sound that makes my heart jump.

'It's great,' I say when the track is over. 'Really, really good. But I can't sing that . . . No way would I remember the words or the tune!'

'We wouldn't expect you to,' Marley says, his eyes blazing now with sudden hope. 'Try. Please. Or sing a song you know – whatever you want! Give us a chance!'

I shake my head. 'No, no, I can't . . .'

In my head, I can hear Mum's voice telling me again and again that music is for losers. I do my best to shake it off.

'Please?' Lexie asks, passing me the written lyrics of the song I've just listened to. 'Try?'

'For me?' Sasha adds. 'So I don't go to my grave carrying all this guilt and regret? Please?'

'A lead singer with a pet magpie could be kind of cool,' Lee adds, reeling me in with his laughing eyes. 'Give it a go? We need you!'

It's a very long time since anyone wanted me on their side, on their team. At Bellvale, I was always the troublemaker, the outsider. I was useful for shaking things up a bit, pushing the boundaries, taking the flak, but nobody actually needed me. I'd probably have let them down anyway, knowing me. I am a disaster waiting to happen – Mum's always said so.

But, in spite of my doubts, I find myself listening to the track again, clutching the lyrics, my guts a tangle of terror and panic. The band set up and play the tune without the words, and then they're ready to go again – with me.

'This is stupid . . . how many times do I have to tell you? No! No way!' I argue, but nobody's even listening except for Lee, who leans forward, takes my hand and gently pulls me over towards the mic. Pie, back on my shoulder in a gesture of solidarity, leans in to chitter encouragingly in my ear.

'Sing,' Lee says, his eyes on mine, smiling as if he knows how scared I am inside. 'Just sing.'

So I do. I open my mouth and the words tumble out. My voice starts out small and unsure, but it builds until the song is big and loud and angry, even though the original was wistful and sad and soft. I sing with everything I have, and the others come in around me with drums, bass, guitar, violin, cello and trumpet. The song builds into something different, something bolder than the original version, and I'm hanging on to the mic and pouring everything I have into it.

When the song is over, Marley runs across and hugs me, which is seriously alarming. Bex and Lee are laughing and the others look slightly stunned.

'Keep going,' Marley says. 'This is awesome. Epic! Incredible! Don't stop, Phoenix, please!'

He throws me the little notebook with the 'Fireworks' song in it, and I sing that to the sixties melody from this morning, with no accompaniment, only a tentative drum beat and a wisp of violin. The others are just staring, grinning, wide-eyed.

I sing some of Grandma Lou's favourite sixties songs, including the Ked Wilder hit 'Phoenix' I loved so much as a little girl, and Marley hands me the lyrics of a few more Lost & Found tracks, and I try those too. They come out differently to the way they are supposed to sound, but nobody seems to mind.

'There is no wrong way to do it,' Marley insists. 'Do it your way, Phoenix. Just sing – we'll fit round you! Keep going! Please!'

We practise until the light falls into inky darkness and Grandma Lou knocks on the railway carriage door to see if I'm there because tea is ready and she hasn't seen me since breakfast.

'I knew you'd do it!' she says, laughing, shaking her head. 'I knew it!'

The band make me promise to come back tomorrow, make me promise I'll stick with them, be one of them, and Pie flies up from my shoulder and does a circuit of the railway carriage, shrieking and swooping in and out of the band members.

I'm high on hot chocolate and happiness and song, and I can't stop smiling.

Diary of Phoenix Marlow, age 11$\frac{1}{2}$

Today I got thrown out of the school choir. I was on stage, waiting for my solo, whispering to Rosalind March about an especially nasty French test when Mum came in through the side door with a face like thunder. She said I was a disruptive influence and didn't deserve to be in the choir because I don't take it seriously. Miss Brown tried to argue, but Mum wouldn't have it. I've been thrown out. I came back to the dorm and cried silently into my pillow for almost an hour, because choir is one of the few things I actually like about Bellvale.

Miss Brown is probably glad to be shot of me, anyhow.

8

Different

On Sunday morning I'm up early, making pancakes for Grandma Lou. I can't remember when I last felt so happy. Yesterday afternoon nobody laughed at my singing. Nobody said I was out of tune or flat or squeaky. Nobody said I was an embarrassment. They hugged me and told me I was awesome, and even though I got some of the words wrong and changed the melodies and timings by accident, nobody seemed to care.

My head whirls with ideas and plans – I want to make pancakes and write songs and sing my heart out, all at once. My face hurts from smiling so much. I turn three cartwheels in a row down the hallway, and come to a halt right in front of the big old mirror that hangs beside the coat stand. My reflection looks surprised, sassy, pink-cheeked. My hair looks like I've just clambered through a holly bush and my green eyes are wide and shining.

I can almost hear Mum's voice telling me I look like a wild thing, and today that makes me smile. So what? When I was little, Mum liked me to keep my hair short. She said it was easier to look after that way, and old photos show me as a freckled kid with bright auburn curls chopped into an awkward bob. I had to keep my hair back with slides and clips to stop it falling into my eyes.

When I started at Bellvale, I refused to have it cut again and over three years it's grown almost to waist length. I hated every tug of the brush or comb when it was short, but these days my hair is my trademark and I look after it properly with conditioner and serum and mousse. The way I see it, people are always going to notice you if you have auburn hair. You might as well give them something to look at, right?

Today, though, I am my true through-a-hedge-backwards self. I stick my tongue out at my reflection, laughing.

I don't look anything like as sad or as angry as the girl who used to look back at me in the mirror at Bellvale. Have I left her behind? Can I be different here, happier? I really hope so.

I trail a fingertip over the mirror's surface, studying the crazed and darkened surface round the edges. Who else has gazed into this glass? Did Grandma Lou ever study her reflection as a teen and wonder how her life would unfold? Could she see adventure, fame and heartache waiting for her? Did my mum stare at her own pinched and frowny face, dreaming of boarding school and Latin lessons and being captain of the hockey team? Probably.

I wonder what the future holds for me. A few days ago I'd have seen nothing but trouble, but now I feel the faintest stirrings of hope.

The kitchen smells of pancakes and coffee by the time Grandma Lou comes down. I sweep her up in a waltz around the room, me in my slipper socks and Grandma Lou in her clunky green suede clogs, before dishing up the pancakes, complete with sugar and lemon juice, the way she always used to do them for me.

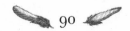

'It was the weirdest thing,' I tell her, for something like the seventieth time. 'Yesterday. They actually liked my voice, even though I don't sound anything like Sasha. I got things wrong and sang things too fast or too slow, or got the words all upside down – but everyone liked it! They even liked the song I wrote that isn't even a real song. And they totally loved Pie!

'I don't get it, Grandma Lou. I keep thinking it's a mistake. They'll wake up this morning and worry about how to break the news to me that I'm not right after all . . .'

My mobile, which has been buzzing all night with messages from the band, bleeps with yet another. This time it's from Lee, telling me he'll see me at rehearsals at eleven, that he's glad I'm the new singer, that I'm cool and brilliant.

I think Lee likes me, and there is definitely something about him that draws me in . . . the cheekbones and the cheeky grin are almost irresistible, but I can't let myself get involved. I've had a few boyfriends – it goes with the bad-girl territory – but it never ends well. They either dump me, because they're trouble and I'm not reckless enough for their tastes, or I dump them because I'm trouble and they're too nice, too kind. I'm pretty sure Lee falls into the second category – too nice, too kind.

I can't get involved, because things will fall apart no matter what I do . . . I always get scared, back off. I don't know if I'm scared of hurting them or scared they might hurt me, but I know I'd mess up and finish things, and then we'd be stuck in the band together and it would be beyond awkward. No, better not to get involved.

I put my phone away with a sigh.

'You'll be perfect,' Grandma Lou is saying. 'Different is good, don't you see? A carbon copy of Sasha would never be as good as Sasha herself – they need someone fresh. You have an amazing voice, a strong, quirky, memorable voice, and that's what they need – the rest is detail. You'll learn the songs, or they'll adapt them to suit you, and you can all move forward together. They're great kids, and so talented . . . and now they've got you, the sky's the limit! I'm so proud of you, Phoenix – it took courage to audition, I know. You put on such a brave face for the world, but inside you're not confident at all, are you?'

I force a smile. 'Better to put on a brave face than show your weaknesses, right? I don't want to be hurt again, Grandma Lou . . .'

My beautiful gran falters, her face suddenly serious. 'What do you mean, sweetheart?' she asks. 'Who hurt you?'

I almost laugh out loud. Where do I start? With parents who didn't love each other enough to stay together? With Dad, who told me he'd always be there for me, then dropped me like a hot potato once Weird Wanda came on the scene? They high-tailed it off to Dubai and proceeded to replace me with two squalling toddlers called Drake and Dara. Dad hardly even bothers to FaceTime now. I'm yesterday's news.

As for Mum, she's colder than the Arctic tundra . . . sometimes I think that disapproval runs through her veins instead of blood. Even if I had burned down the school, it wouldn't have warmed her up.

'Dad . . . and Mum . . .' I whisper. 'Same old, same old.'

Grandma Lou looks stricken.

'Perhaps we're all doomed to hurt the people we love the most,' she says. 'When Vivi was a child, I'd have done anything for her, anything at all – but I didn't understand her. Instead, I saw some version of how I had been at that age, a child who loved freedom, travel, art, music. I thought I'd given Vivi an idyllic childhood, but she didn't see it like that. She wanted routine and boundaries, the things I couldn't give her.

'By the time she was ten, she was campaigning to go to boarding school. We looked at some wonderful artsy ones, but Vivi picked out the strictest school ever. She was top of the class in her all her subjects and winning cups for lacrosse and hockey, and she started asking me not to come to collect her on open days, because people might know who I was, or they might laugh at my funny clothes and the way I did my hair . . .'

'Oh, Grandma Lou!' I say.

She sighs. 'Well, teenagers can get very hung up about that kind of thing. No matter how hard I tried, I never managed to rebuild things between us. Do you want some life advice, Phoenix? If you get a chance to build bridges, repair something broken . . . just do it. Do it, because you'll never regret it.

'I did my best, and I suspect Vivi thinks she's doing the best for you too. She loves you very much, Phoenix – but somehow she doesn't know how to show it!'

She folds her arms round me and holds me tight. Maybe it's enough to have one person who loves you, one person who understands you and is always on your side. I have Grandma Lou, and that counts for a lot.

'Grandma Lou . . . why did you and Mum fall out?' I ask. 'We used to spend lots of time here, until I was ten or so. I know you sent cards and presents at Christmas and on my birthday, but I sent you two letters and you never replied . . .'

'I didn't get any letters,' Grandma Lou says with a frown. 'But I did write . . . oh dear!'

'Mum must have binned them,' I realize. 'Why would she do that? What went wrong?'

Grandma Lou's eyes shine with sadness. 'Oh, it's a long story,' she says, stacking up plates and taking them to the sink. 'I'll tell you another time. Now, I need to get to my studio, and you've got rehearsal at eleven . . . Can you fix yourself a snack for lunch? I'll see you later!'

I'm clearly not the only one who puts on a brave face and keeps things hidden in this family, and while my gran, my mum and I may be very different characters, we all share one common trait. We're stubborn to the core, every one of us.

*

By ten to eleven, me and Pie head across to the old railway carriage. Marley is already there, and while it's quiet my doubts spill out.

'Marley . . . are you sure I'm the right person for this? I haven't sung in front of people for years – and I can't sing things the way you want, no matter how hard I try . . .'

He dismisses my questions with a wave of his hand. 'You're totally the right person. We'll adapt to your style, Phoenix, because it's weird and unique and brilliant. You'll learn to sing in public – we can set up some small gigs to get you used to it. You won't mess up or let anyone down – you're going to take us to the top!'

'What if you're wrong?' I argue.

'I'm never wrong,' he says. 'Look, are you willing to work at this?'

'Of course!'

'Well then. Do your best and you won't let us down. Sorted!'

I fill the kettle and Marley cleans out the wood burner, and by the time the others arrive the fire is alight, the kettle has boiled and mugs of hot chocolate are lined up along the countertop.

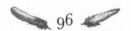

'Today will be hard work,' Marley announces. 'We have a lot to do if we want to come together as a band – this is a big change for us, but I think we're all agreed it is a positive one. I've reworked the melodies for a couple of the songs Phoenix tried yesterday, bringing things more in line with her style. We'll all have to adjust a bit, change our accompaniments maybe, but it'll be worth it . . . We're stepping up to the next level!'

The next few hours pass in a chaotic tangle of noise. It's like being in the eye of a particularly violent storm, but, as the hours pass, the chaos subsides and something beautiful begins to emerge.

'Try "Song for the Sea" again,' Marley tells me. 'Sami, bring the flute in earlier – I want that as the backdrop to everything. Happi, Romy, George, go louder with the strings – and, Dylan, pull back on the drums, think of crashing waves and driving rain . . . good! Brilliant!'

On we go to 'Mask', a song that Marley is happy to smash to bits and rebuild from scratch.

'Listen to Phoenix,' he instructs. 'She makes the lyrics fierce and strong and powerful! Use that as your framework . . . Less cello, George. Less flute. Actually, no flute on this, Sami. Lee, I want your brass section to be euphoric – uplifting – go loud! Keep singing, Phoenix!'

At two o'clock Jake and Sami slip out to the chippy, coming back with a feast for the band to share. Pie clears up the leftovers, then ducks out of the window to watch the rest of the practice from the branches of a nearby tree.

We push on again, and by the end of the day we have two songs sounding strong, and another couple on the way. I'm so high on the buzz of it all I might never come down.

'Was I right, or was I right?' Marley crows. 'This is something special . . . something different!'

'Maybe it's not too late to get Ked Wilder back in the game?' Bex muses. 'I'd love to hear his feedback on this!'

'Just you wait,' Marley says to me. 'This is only the beginning . . .'

Diary of Phoenix Marlow, age 10

We've just come back from Grandma Lou's house. Something bad happened, I don't know what, and now Mum is not speaking to Grandma Lou. Ever again. Mum was very cross and Grandma Lou was crying and nobody would tell me what was wrong, and we packed our bags three days early and drove back up to Scotland. Mum said we didn't need Grandma Lou anyway because we had each other, but I don't think that's true because Mum is usually too busy to bother with me. Mum says we'll be fine on our own, but I am missing Grandma Lou already.

9

Famous

On Monday a posse of Year Seven girls ambush me by the school lockers and ask for an autograph.

'What for?' I ask, which is clearly the wrong thing to say.

'Because you're the new lead singer with the Lost & Found,' one of the girls says patiently, as if explaining to a very small child. 'We are the band's biggest fans. We follow their Instagram and Facebook pages, so we saw the news straight away. You're famous!'

She holds out a mobile phone with a picture of me singing in the old railway carriage, Pie perched on my shoulder. The picture was posted yesterday evening, and

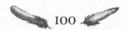

has almost four hundred likes and a whole slew of comments. I grit my teeth and resolve to have a sharp word with Marley about posting stuff without asking . . . but maybe this is part of being in a band?

'Is it true you've moved from New York specially to be in the band?' the littlest girl asks.

'Is it true you used to be a child star in Hollywood?'

'Is it true Ked Wilder heard you sing on YouTube and asked you to join the Lost & Found?'

'No, no and no,' I say, scribbling a signature on the open jotters being pushed at me. 'I auditioned, like everyone else, and they gave me a go.'

'Can we have a selfie?'

Seriously, this never happened at Bellvale. I strike a pose for the Year Sevens, then make a hasty escape – only to walk right into an older boy with dark eyes and a carefully gelled quiff. I almost tip an armful of books on the floor, and he puts out an arm to steady me.

'Just like in the movies,' Sharleen Scott says scathingly as she struts past, ponytail swinging, but she has a point because it actually is, a bit.

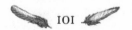

'Phoenix Marlow, right?' the boy says with a lazy smile. 'Millford's newest star!'

'Ha. I'm guessing nothing much happens here, right?'

'Oh, you'd be surprised,' he says. 'My name's Matt Brennan, I'm in Year Eleven. I used to run the school magazine, but I've stepped down to focus on GCSEs, otherwise I'd be chasing you for an exclusive interview. Who knows, maybe I'll chase you anyway . . . old habits die hard. See you around!'

He's off, stalking along the corridor, and I head to maths with a smile on my face. Matt Brennan has that artfully careless sort of style that takes hard work, hard cash and hours in front of the mirror to perfect, and my instincts tell me he's definitely not too nice or too kind. If I'm not mistaken, he's trouble, and even though I'm trying to steer clear of that here, the pull of it is almost magnetic.

Boys. They are a whole lot more complicated than you'd think.

I'm pretty hyper all through lunch, doing a little low-level flirting with Lee and wondering what's actually so wrong with 'nice' and 'kind'. Is it because I think I don't deserve those things? Lexie and Sami are clearly a couple, and so are Jake and Sasha, and they seem happy enough without the drama of cheats, liars and losers in the equation. To me, though, it seems scary. A bad boy can't hurt me because I know in advance he's trouble and I'd never let myself fall for him. A nice boy is a whole different thing, and way more dangerous for the heart.

After lunch, it's time for ritual torture, otherwise known as hockey. Bellvale has trained me to be tough and fearless on the hockey pitch, and Sasha and Romy are in my team, which makes for a few laughs along the way. I score three goals without even trying and later, once I've showered and changed, Ms Trent calls me into her office.

She thinks I'm a natural and wants me in the school Under-15s team without delay. 'I don't really like hockey,' I tell her, and she grits her teeth and explains that 'like' doesn't come into it.

'Where's your team spirit?' she wants to know. 'Your loyalty to the school?'

'I don't have any,' I explain brightly. 'It's hard enough looking after myself without having anyone else to worry about!'

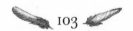 103

She arranges her face into a frowny, disapproving expression, but that doesn't scare me. I've lived with Mum for long enough – I've seen far worse.

'I find your attitude baffling,' she says. 'I do hope you'll think again about this, Phoenix. Staying on the sidelines of life may be safe, but it's also rather lonely, and a terrible waste of potential.'

This comment is worryingly accurate, but now is not the time to update her on my life history or explain why I find it hard to trust people or hold on to friendships for long.

'If you change your mind, we have practice after school on Mondays and Fridays,' Ms Trent says with a sigh.

'I have band practice those days,' I say politely. 'But thanks!'

By the time I make my escape, Sasha and Romy are long gone, and I take a wrong turn and end up on a shady, neglected pathway between the gym and the perimeter fence. Stopping to retrace my steps, I glimpse Sharleen Scott skulking behind a holly bush, hunched over, a thin plume of smoke rising from her cupped hands.

Smokers' corner . . . every school has one, I guess – a place where kids can hide out and skive lessons without

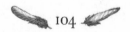

even leaving the school grounds. I've been there, done that . . . but my flirtation with yellow fingers and a hacking cough was thankfully short-lived.

I should walk away, leave Sharleen to stew in her own spiteful juices, but something stops me. How many times have I been the outsider kid, the angry kid, the lost kid? How many times have I hidden myself away behind dustbins or sheds, looking for somewhere quiet to chill or rage or let the tears come? More than I care to remember.

Sharleen warned me to watch my back, but I don't plan to go through life looking over my shoulder in fear of approaching trouble. I'd rather face it head on. And, of course, there's Grandma Lou's life advice about building bridges.

I step closer, and Sharleen looks up, her face moving from startled to sneering in two seconds flat. 'What d'you want, new girl?' she says. 'Come to gloat because you got through the audition and I didn't? Well done. Today Millford, tomorrow the world, huh?'

'Why do we have to be enemies, Sharleen?' I ask. 'What have I ever done to you?'

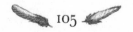

She laughs. 'You're not listening, are you? You took my chance of fame and fortune. It's not even a big deal to you, is it?'

'It kind of is,' I tell her. 'But yeah, whatever. We don't always get what we want in this life, do we?'

'I bet you do,' Sharleen says. 'Turns out you're that mad old artist lady's grandkid. I reckon you've probably had everything you ever wanted served up to you on a silver platter. Poor little rich girl, huh?'

'You're wrong,' I say. 'You have no idea how wrong.'

'Am I, though?' she challenges. 'Ever been hungry, Phoenix? So hungry your stomach hurts? Ever had to get your clothes from a charity shop or lost your home and had to kip three to a room in a stinking B & B with mould on the walls? Ever had to survive on food bank handouts? I don't think so. You wouldn't survive a single day.'

I don't have a smart comeback to this, or any comeback at all.

'Oh,' I say. 'I . . . no, I've never had to live like that.'

'What do you care, anyway?' she asks.

'Who says I care?'

The bell rings to signal the start of the next lesson, but neither of us move.

'Best get to class, new girl, or you'll be in trouble. Don't wanna get told off in your first week, do you?' she says.

'Don't much care,' I reply, pushing away the thought that I should be in class, that I'm supposed to be turning over a new leaf. Being good all the time is tiring, and, besides, something about Sharleen makes me want to stay. 'What lesson have you got?'

'Music. Me mates are skiving school today, so there's nobody to mess around with, and the teacher's off too, so it's not like I'm missing anything.'

I sit down on an old tree stump. Sharleen is shivering slightly in a thin cotton jacket, and she's wearing worn-out canvas flats even though it's November. I can see that, to her, I might seem like a girl who has everything. It's a bit of a reality check, really.

No matter how different our backgrounds may be, I know the look in Sharleen's eyes, that sad, empty gaze that ignites all too easily into anger. I know it well, because I saw it every morning for years when I looked in the mirror.

We have more in common than you'd think, Sharleen and me.

'You're doing GCSE music, right? Exams next summer? You could try for a performing arts course after school . . .'

'I'm not clever enough,' Sharleen says. 'College is for posh kids!'

'Rubbish,' I tell her. 'You get on to a course like that on ability. You're into singing . . .'

'I'm no good at it,' she says in a small voice. 'Even my music teacher says so. Should have stuck to dance. I had lessons when I was little, got solos in all the shows . . . then Dad left and everything went pear-shaped.'

'Dance, then. If you had a skill then, you'll still have it . . . and I know you're good at drama because you do a great job of stomping about the school acting hard.'

'You think it's an act?'

'Of course it is,' I say. 'I've been doing the same thing for years – I know all the tricks. Oh, except the one where you trip the new kid up in the lunch hall. That was pretty hardcore.'

'Yeah . . . sorry about that,' Sharleen says. 'I wanted to make it clear I was top dog, that's all.'

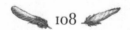

'I don't care about being top dog,' I tell her. 'I just want to be left alone.'

'Whatever,' she says. 'Want a ciggy?'

'No thanks. Bad for the voice . . . and who wants yellow fingers? I've got some chocolate, though . . .'

Sharleen says something unprintable and blows smoke in my face, but I don't flinch, and she laughs. 'Give us some chocolate, then! You think there's one of those performing arts courses in Millford?'

'Bound to be,' I say. 'I'll google it for you if you like . . .'

We sit for a while in silence while I scroll through the internet, finding performing arts courses in Millford and Birmingham. Sharleen's face has lost its pinched, sour look, and there's the faintest flicker of excitement in her eyes.

We're still huddled together, Sharleen blowing smoke rings and telling me to steer clear of Matt Brennan, when a stern voice interrupts us.

'Well, well, well,' Mr Simpson says. 'If it isn't Sharleen Scott . . . and our new Year Nine girl, if I'm not mistaken. Shouldn't you two be in class?'

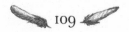

Sharleen scrambles to put out her ciggy and I'm on my feet, reeling off some ridiculous excuse about getting lost on the way to lessons.

'Sharleen was helping me, sir,' I say. 'I thought this might be a shortcut to the science lab, but Sharleen said not, and then I had a bit of a dizzy spell and had to sit down for a minute . . . She was just looking after me.'

'Is that so?' Mr Simpson says. 'You've been sitting here for forty minutes, ever since the bell for class went, is that right? Some dizzy spell!'

I shrug, and Mr Simpson turns to Sharleen, who is looking very red-faced now. 'And what's your excuse?'

Unable to hold it in any longer, Sharleen opens her mouth and a plume of smoke leaks out, as if she is a small, hard-faced dragon with a blonde ponytail, breathing fire and fury.

'Right!' Mr Simpson barks. 'My office, now, the pair of you!'

I think my run of good luck is over.

Diary of Phoenix Marlow, age 13

Last night I sneaked out of the dorm after lights out and met Arran McAllister down in the village. We shared a bag of chips and walked around the streets for a bit, then he kissed me. It wasn't really like in the movies, more like trying to eat a plateful of cold spaghetti without getting the sauce all over your face. I asked if that meant we were dating and Arran said he isn't a one-girl sort of boy, so that's that. I didn't really like him anyway. Well, I did a bit.

10

Trouble

I guess I should have expected it. I've turned over enough new leaves in the past fourteen years to plant an entire forest. Sabotaging myself is a skill I have definitely perfected over the years.

'Ta for trying to take the blame,' Sharleen says. 'Sorry for dropping you in it.'

I shrug. I know well enough that my own bad choices brought me here.

Mr Simpson lectures us on the dangers of smoking and the evils of skipping lessons, and I want to tell him I'm sorry and that I'd never smoke and didn't actually plan to skive off science, but he isn't really in a listening mood. I want to ask for a second chance, to beg him not to phone my gran, but I'm too proud. Instead I fix a defiant look on my face and pretend I don't care.

'It's not the first run in I've had with you, Sharleen, and I'm sure it won't be the last,' he says wearily. 'You, though, Phoenix . . . you've only been here a couple of days, and already you're in trouble. I suggest you choose your friends a little more carefully from now on. I have to say I'm very disappointed in you.'

That's me, endlessly disappointing to everyone.

The school bell peals out and I move to pick up my rucksack, but Mr Simpson laughs.

'Not so fast,' he says. 'You're both in detention until four o'clock. Sharleen, you'll be writing an essay on the dangers of smoking. Phoenix, you'll be writing about the importance of attending lessons and following school rules.'

'Awesome,' Sharleen drawls, but I'm starting to feel sick. I have band practice right after school – I can't miss it. Messing up at school is bad, but messing up with the Lost & Found is worse. They wanted me, worked so hard to get me involved . . . and already I'm letting them down.

Shame and anger battle it out inside me.

'You can't keep us in after school without warning,' I argue. 'It's against our basic human rights! Or something . . .'

'I think you'll find I can, actually,' Mr Simpson growls. 'You waste my time, I'll waste yours. Seems fair to me.'

'But . . . there's somewhere else I have to be! It's important!'

'So is your school career,' he snaps. 'You should have thought of that before you decided to break the rules. I'm not happy with your attitude, Phoenix, not one bit. I'm putting you both on report for a fortnight and I'll be keeping a very close eye on your behaviour, but right now you are going to room 15 to write those essays!'

I stomp into the classroom, Sharleen trailing in my wake.

I'm halfway through the first page of an essay on how school rules stifle creativity and imagination when my mobile buzzes quietly from my blazer pocket, and I take a sneaky look under the desk. It's a message from Lee, asking if I'm OK and if I've forgotten we've got band practice.

'Something's come up. I'll be there by ten past four,' I text back.

Moments later, there's a reply: **Marley's not happy.**

Well, too bad – neither am I. Mr Simpson, sitting behind the teacher's desk with his laptop, holds my future in his hands – one call to Grandma Lou or Mum and all my attempts at a semi-normal teenage life could be over. Mum would have me enrolled in some high-security boot-camp boarding school before I could get my bags packed.

Mr Simpson releases us into the wild at 4 p.m. precisely. 'I won't call your grandmother,' he tells me as I hand in my essay. 'Not this time. But I'll be looking for a marked improvement in both behaviour and attitude, Phoenix.'

He doesn't say anything to Sharleen. I get the impression he gave up on her some time ago.

We part at the school gates, bonded by detention and disgrace. 'You're OK for a posh kid,' she says, and coming from Sharleen that's praise indeed.

I race across the park, backpack swinging. Pie meets me midway, flying ahead and cawing encouragement. I arrive at the old railway carriage at ten past four exactly, red-faced, panting and ready with a sob story about Mr Simpson's control-freakery. The rest of the band make sympathetic noises, but Marley is stony-faced.

'Detention?' he echoes. 'Seriously? This is your second ever official practice with the Lost & Found, and you keep us waiting because you had detention?'

'I didn't mean it to happen,' I argue. 'Obviously! It was all a misunderstanding . . .'

'The only misunderstanding was that I believed you when you said you were willing to put the work in,' Marley says.

'Everyone makes mistakes,' Bex cuts in. 'It's no biggie, Marley. Let's not waste time arguing!'

'Waste time?' Marley roars. 'What d'you think we've been doing? The Lost & Found isn't just any old band – it's a band on the brink of success, and Phoenix doesn't seem to get that . . .'

That's the last straw, and my temper flares.

'You know what I do get, Marley?' I snap. 'I get that you bullied me into joining this band even though you knew I didn't want to. I told you I was trouble, and you said it didn't matter. Well, looks like it does matter after all. Stuff your poxy band! I don't need it!'

I turn on my heel and leg it back across the grass, ignoring the calls and yells of the others. If I go back to

Greystones, they'll follow me there, so I run along the street in the fading light, heading for the park, looking for solitude so I can let the tears come. Unfortunately for me, solitude seems to be off the menu today.

At the park gates I run right into Matt Brennan, the Year Eleven boy with the quiff, and he grabs my arm as I try to dodge past him.

'Phoenix?' he says, clocking that I'm upset. 'Hey, what's the matter? Trouble with the band?'

'You could say that,' I mutter, shaking free of his grip and checking over my shoulder in case anyone is trailing me. 'Look, I need to get out of here . . .'

'No worries,' he says, hooking an arm through mine. 'I've just come from photography club, but I could use a hot chocolate right now, if you fancy one. I'm a good listener!'

My shoulders slump. I'm supposed to be through with bad boys, but what's the point when my life is an ongoing disaster movie? I may as well give in and accept it.

'OK,' I tell him. 'Let's go, before they find me!'

Ten minutes later we are sitting at a corner table in the Leaping Llama, Millford's one and only hipster cafe,

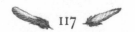

where the waiters are all painfully cool, with beards, brogues, vintage waistcoats and narrow trousers that seem to have shrunk in the wash. Matt orders luxury hot chocolates with whipped cream and dipping flakes, then drapes an unwanted arm round my shoulders. I scoot my chair back and wriggle free.

'Let me guess – the Lost & Found honeymoon is over already?' he asks, running a hand over that perfectly gelled quiff. 'What happened?'

'I had a row with Marley,' I say. 'I was late to rehearsal, and he wasn't exactly understanding about it . . .'

'No, he wouldn't be,' Matt says. 'He's a total waste of space!'

'Yeah, well, I think I quit the band,' I tell him. 'Must be a record for the fastest turnover of a lead singer, huh?'

Matt's eyes narrow, and a wolfish grin lights up his face. 'You quit? Wow – that's a bit of a scoop! You're probably not their biggest fan right now, huh?'

'Not exactly,' I admit.

'I think a lot of people would love to know the inside story of the band,' Matt says. 'They've been so hyped,

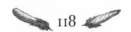

and that creepy old pop star Ked Wilder took them under his wing.'

'Creepy?' I echo. 'He's my gran's friend. What's creepy about him?'

'You tell me,' Matt presses. 'Why does an old pop star want to hang around a bunch of teenagers? Weird if you ask me!'

'He was trying to help the band,' I explain, slightly irritated now. 'My gran got him involved. Nothing creepy about that!'

Matt changes tack. 'Maybe you're right,' he concedes. 'Maybe it's more Marley's ruthless streak that rings alarm bells with me. You can be honest, Phoenix – did Marley bully you? Because I hear that's why Sasha left . . .'

I frown. 'What's all this about, Matt? Sasha had her own reasons for leaving, but bullying wasn't one of them. I don't have any juicy gossip on the Lost & Found, and, even if I did, I wouldn't be telling you!'

Matt's face falls. 'Look, I'm planning a career in journalism,' he says. 'I'd love to get a scoop on the band into the national press – I'll keep your name out of it, if you prefer – and all publicity is good publicity, right?'

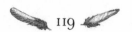

I've dated enough low-life bad boys to recognize a liar when I meet one, and I'm losing patience with Matt Brennan. I may be cross with Marley, but I'd never gossip about the band to anyone, let alone this smarmy loser.

'I don't think so, Matt,' I say. 'Thanks for the hot chocolate, but I won't be dishing the dirt on my friends, OK?'

'Friends?' he says. 'I thought you said you'd quit?'

'I say a lot of things,' I tell him. 'You don't want to believe everything you hear!'

Matt's face hardens, and he says something unrepeatable. I just smile to show him I don't care, and at that moment Lee appears in the cafe doorway. 'She's here!' he yells back into the street, and Marley piles in after him.

The smile slides right off Lee's face when he spots Matt. 'What are you doing with him?' he asks, his lip curling in disgust. 'He's a jerk!'

'Yeah, I worked that out,' I reply.

Matt gets to his feet, scowling. 'Don't believe a word these guys say about me,' he says. 'It's all lies.' He shoves past Marley and Lee and slams out of the cafe. What a charmer . . . next time, maybe I'll listen to Sharleen.

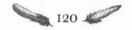

'International Rescue at your service,' Lee says, flopping down into the seat beside me. 'We looked everywhere for you!'

'I was here,' I sulk. 'And I didn't need rescuing!'

A little bit of me can't help liking the fact that Lee and Marley chased after me, all the same. I'm not used to feeling wanted.

'You kind of did, if you ended up with Matt Brennan,' Lee points out. 'He's vile. But this wasn't meant to be a rescue so much as a peace mission . . . Marley?'

Marley drops to his knees beside me, snatching a sprig of berried greenery from the jam jar on the table and clamping it between his teeth. He opens his arms wide, drawing the attention of nearby diners.

'I am a snivelling, wretched fool,' he begins, the words slightly slurred because of the sprig of greenery in his mouth. 'I grovel at your feet for forgiveness . . .'

'Marley, pack it in!'

'I was out of order,' he announces to the cafe at large. 'I let my temper get the better of me. I myself have fallen foul of Mr Simpson too many times to count . . .'

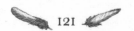

'Get up, Marley!' I hiss, but I'm struggling to suppress a smile.

'Not until you promise you forgive me!'

I roll my eyes. 'I lost my temper too,' I admit. 'And I don't really want to quit. I was upset about the detention and I didn't like being yelled at!'

'I know, I know,' Marley says, holding out the sprig of greenery. 'I was an idiot. Take this as a token of my undying regret and sorrow!'

'No thanks, it's been in your mouth!' I retort, and Marley shrugs and dumps it back in the jam-jar vase.

'I'm going to get hot chocolates,' he decrees. 'To celebrate the fact that I haven't driven away the best teen singer I've ever heard in my whole life. D'you want another?'

'Please . . . this one's cold now!'

Marley laughs and Lee grins his lopsided grin, and all is right with the world again.

Diary of Phoenix Marlow, age $11^3/4$

Today my best friend Lucy told me she didn't want to be best friends any more. She still liked me, she said, but sometimes I could be 'too much'. This is what Mum says about me, and what my other long-lost best friends Jayde, Polly, Amelia and Sarita said. I'm 'too much'. Is it better than being 'not enough'? I have no way of knowing.

I wrote a letter to Grandma Lou last week, but I didn't have a stamp so Mum said she'd post it for me. I haven't had a reply, so it looks like I'm 'too much' for her as well.

11

Too Much

Lee taps out a hasty text message and presses send. 'Don't worry – I'm letting the others know we found you, and that you're still in the band,' he tells me, watching Marley approach the counter. 'He really is upset about scaring you off, y'know. The rest of us are so used to his megalomaniac ways, we try to ignore it when he goes into meltdown. It's about time someone stood up to him!'

'I was out of order too,' I say sadly.

'Nah, just unlucky,' Lee tells me. 'Um . . . how come you were with Matt Brennan?'

I shrug. 'I ran into him by the park gates and he asked me for a hot chocolate,' I explain. 'Turns out he's another weirdo. He was asking me all these questions about Marley and the band. I don't think he likes you guys much!'

Lee frowns. 'He hates us. He used to go out with Sasha, and he conned his way down to Devon at half-term, when we were working with Ked Wilder. He wrote a whole load of lies and sold the piece to one of the tabloid newspapers!'

I'm horrified. 'What? Wow! I didn't tell him anything, though . . . not really. I'm used to seeing myself as the black sheep of the family, but I'm practically an angel compared with Matt Brennan!'

'Who said you were a black sheep?' Lee asks. 'I think you're great!'

'Yeah, but you don't know me,' I point out. 'I'm trouble, too full-on, too hot tempered, too impulsive, too clumsy, too loud . . . too everything. I'm . . . too much.'

Lee's ears glow pink underneath his battered trilby hat. 'Nah, I don't reckon you're too much,' he says. 'Not too much at all. I think you're just right!'

I laugh, but I'm secretly pleased.

'Before the Lost & Found, I was in trouble a lot,' he tells me. 'The teachers used to say I was "too much", too. I have ADHD, and I used to find it hard to settle to

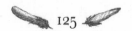

anything. The teachers say I disrupt stuff. I don't mean to, though – I just hate staying still. Being in the band has helped ... finally I have something I can focus on, something I can pour my energy into!'

'That's cool,' I tell him, and he grins that cheeky, lopsided grin.

'You're cool,' he counters. 'Most people don't get me, but you ... maybe you do. I have all this energy coiled up inside me, and so many things I want to do – play in the band, travel the world, have adventures, ask the new girl with hair like spun copper if she'll come on a date ... OK, so I am definitely talking too much now. Sorry! I do that when I get nervous!'

I can't meet his eye.

I like Lee – I like the way he dances about when he plays the trumpet, the kind of fancy footwork that looks effortless and cool and fun. It's like the music is in his soul and he can't stay still, even for a moment. I like his kindness – in the lunch queue with Sharleen Scott on my first day, or when he slips a foil-wrapped square of chocolate into my blazer pocket and winks. I like the way his ears go pink when he's embarrassed, and the way my tummy fills with butterflies when he looks at me.

I just can't go out with him.

Lee is too nice, and anytime I go near that I spoil it. I'd hurt him, let him down, make him hate me. Even if that didn't happen, it would still end in tears. Lee would suss that I was trouble, dump me for someone else and leave me heartbroken. If I'm honest, that's the scenario that scares me most.

I don't think I can handle any more hurt in this lifetime.

'What's taking Marley so long?' I ask, changing the subject. 'He's been ages!'

'He's chatting up the waiter,' Lee tells me. 'Look!'

At the counter, Marley is talking to an older boy in shirt and braces. They're deep in conversation and Marley is laughing a lot and raking a hand through his hair as the boy lines up the hot chocolates and piles on extra cream and marshmallows. It all looks very flirty.

'I think you're right,' I whisper. 'Love's young dream, huh? I didn't realize Marley liked boys . . . I guess he has a soft side after all!'

'Who said romance was dead?' Lee quips.

'Not dead, but definitely overrated,' I say.

There's an awkward silence. 'I really like you, y'know,' Lee says. 'Do you think you'll ever go on a date with me?'

'It might be a long wait!'

'I like a challenge,' he says, and I can't help but laugh.

A week later, my shaky start in the Lost & Found is all but forgotten. I've been on time for every rehearsal, practised every song until I'm word perfect and have even dared to hand over a couple more poems for Marley to turn into songs.

'The thing is, we've known him longer than you,' Bex tells me, mixing cerise hair dye into a paste as I sit on the edge of the bath at Greystones, waiting for her to work some magic. 'He thinks that we're all as obsessed with the Lost & Found as he is. He forgets that some of us actually have a life!'

'I think my temper has the same short fuse as Marley's,' I admit. 'I'm working on it, though! And to be fair, the band is awesome . . . I'm stoked to be a part of it!'

'Me too,' Bex says. 'I'm liking it even more, lately, too – you're taking the sound in a slightly different direction. It's louder, livelier. Not punkier exactly, but there's a really good energy! With Sasha, we were a little bit softer, folkier . . .'

I frown. 'I didn't mean to change things,' I say.

'Of course not, but things are bound to be different now,' Bex argues. 'I can't wait to see what our fans make of it!'

'I'm not ready to test that out just yet!'

'I know,' Bex says. 'Right – let's do this! Dip-dyed hair, Phoenix-style! Cerise into orange into auburn! Sure you still want me to go ahead?'

'You bet,' I tell her. 'You've already bleached the ends – no way are you leaving it like this!'

'It's going to look awesome,' Bex promises, painting orange dye on my hair and stuffing the ends into her bowl of cerise paste. 'I'm an expert at this. You're going to look even more like a phoenix now! Such a cool name . . . were you named after that Ked Wilder song?'

'Maybe – Mum used to like it, I know that much,' I say. 'But she has this phoenix necklace, and I think I was named after that. Grandma Lou gave it to her on her sixteenth birthday, and when I was ten she got me a phoenix charm bracelet to match . . .' I show her my wrist.

'Aww,' Bex says. 'It's beautiful! Your gran's so cool and eccentric. I bet your mum's amazing too . . .'

'Grandma Lou's the normal one,' I say. 'My mum is so cold you'd catch frostbite if you went too near. Then there's my wicked stepmother, who put a spell on my dad so he'd forget he actually has a daughter. As for Drake and Dara . . .'

'Are they dogs?' Bex asks.

'No, half-brothers,' I say sadly.

'Well, that's families,' Bex says, and I shut up then because I know she and Lexie are in foster care, which means they have their own messed-up family stories too. Then there's Sami, who lost his dad on the journey from Syria, and Romy, who looks after her disabled mum with no dad on the scene – and even Marley and Dylan whose dad also seems to be out of the picture. I know that no matter how odd and mixed up my family is, I'm lucky to have them, and lucky too not to have to use food banks like Sharleen and her family.

'Don't worry, Phoenix, you've always got us,' Bex is saying. 'The Lost & Found is like a family, right? And I think Lee has a crush on you . . . Wait till he sees your new hair!'

I smile. 'Lee's really nice. I do quite fancy him, but I don't want to get involved right now. I don't have a great track record with boys . . . They end up getting hurt, or I do. Besides, it can't be a great idea to go out with someone in the band, right? Wouldn't it all get a bit heavy?'

Bex raises an eyebrow. 'It works for Lexie and Sami,' she points out. 'Jake and Sasha too, although neither of them are actually in the band, technically. I think Romy quite liked George too, but nothing's come of that one. I think she scares him a bit . . . she's gained so much confidence lately. She used to be really shy, but now she's found her style and her self-esteem, and maybe that's too much for George.'

'Too much . . .' I echo. 'Yeah, I've had that trouble myself. How come girls who break the rules or dare to stick up for themselves are "too much"? I dunno about too much – I reckon Romy's too good for George!'

'I do, too,' Bex agrees. 'Lately I'm not sure that George's heart has been in the band, to be honest.'

'I know,' I agree. 'What about you, Bex? Any romance on the horizon?'

She laughs. 'Not a chance. I have more than enough on my plate with schoolwork and the band . . . for now, at least. Anyway . . . time to wash this off and see what we've got!'

I lean over the bath as Bex rinses the colour away, conditions and rinses again. She chills for a while with a GCSE English text while I dry my hair, and the two of us examine the results in my dressing-table mirror.

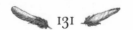

Bex is a fierce teen punk goddess with a razor-sharp intellect, but she's also the best amateur hairdresser I've ever met. My hair looks awesome . . . a blaze of cerise and orange blending seamlessly into natural auburn. What with the ringlet curls, I am a living, breathing bonfire.

'My mum would disown me if she saw this,' I say, grinning a little at the thought of it. 'She'd say it was a disgrace!'

'Sounds like a win to me,' Bex says.

'I don't know,' I say, shaking my hair and checking the mirror again. 'Really? Are you sure it's not too much?'

Bex rolls her eyes. 'Phoenix, when are you going to learn? Too much is exactly the look we're going for!' I smile and slip the torn-off front of the hair dye boxes into my Quality Street tin.

The dip-dyed hair is a hit with Grandma Lou and the Lost & Found, although at school it earns me a talking-to from Mr Simpson. 'I'm a little concerned that you're trying to push the boundaries here,' he says.

'I am,' I tell him, and he puts me on report for another week.

Diary of Phoenix Marlow, age 12

Today is Mother's Day. I gave Mum a card I'd
painted, taken from an old photo of her when she was
little, dressed in an embroidered tunic in Marrakesh.
She's laughing, her freckled face turned up to the sun.
I love the picture because I've never seen Mum look
this happy in all the time I've known her.

I spent weeks on my painting, and instead of the
usual Mother's Day greeting inside, I wrote that we
should take a trip to Marrakesh one day, together. I'd
give anything to see my mum laugh like the little girl
in the photo.

Surprise, surprise - Mum hated it. She wrinkled
up her nose and said, 'Good grief, Phoenix, don't be
so ridiculous,' and instead of putting the card on her
desk or even on the mantelpiece she stuffed it into a
drawer.

Suppose I should be grateful she didn't throw it
straight in the bin.

12

Marley's Confession

As Saturday's practice crashes to a halt, Marley announces that he has news. 'Just some band business before you all head home,' he says. 'Shall we go to the Leaping Llama? I'll stand everyone a hot chocolate out of the band's petty cash!'

We head out into the fading light, Pie perched on my shoulder as usual.

'What's the big news then, Marley?' Bex demands as we walk. 'Should I be worried that you think we need sweetening up with hot chocolate first?'

'Trust me,' Marley says. 'It's good news, promise!'

Lee falls into step with me. 'Did I tell you how much I like your hair?' he asks, his ears pink beneath the battered trilby.

'Once or twice,' I say with a grin. 'It's OK – you can tell me again!'

'I like your hair,' he repeats. 'I liked it before and I like it now. You look like a fiery warrior princess! You could come out with me sometime and I can tell you all this some more?'

'I'll think about it,' I say, and Lee grins at me from behind a messy fall of hair. I badly want to reach out and tuck it behind his ears.

'At least Pie appreciates me,' Lee says, as the magpie hops from my shoulder to his. 'He clearly has great taste –'

Without warning, Pie grabs Lee's battered trilby and disappears into the darkening sky with it.

'Hey!' he yells. 'Stop! Thief!' Even though Lee gives chase, he doesn't stand a chance, and eventually gives up, laughing.

'He must have wanted the feathers!' I say. 'He doesn't normally do stuff like that!'

'Scoundrels, the pair of you,' Lee says.

The Leaping Llama is all lit up with fairy lights and as we push through the door both a blast of warm air and a blast of cool music greet us. The place is busy, but the young waiter who Marley was flirting with on my last visit rushes over and quickly moves two tables together to make a space for us. 'Millford's coolest band is always welcome here,' he says. 'I'm definitely a fan. Enjoy!'

We arrange ourselves round the tables, which on closer inspection turn out to be ancient school desks complete with old inkwells and Latin graffiti inscribed into the wood, while Marley heads to the counter to order.

'He's definitely up to something,' Bex says with a frown. 'Marley never dips into petty cash if he can help it . . .'

I think Marley's just looking for another excuse to see the flirty waiter, but what do I know?

'At least we get hot chocolate,' I say. 'And brownies, by the look of it!'

The young waiter sets down a tray of hot chocolates, piled high with cream and cinnamon, each with a chocolate flake to stir. The brownies are squishy and vegan, and come with ice cream on the side. Lee scoops up a spoonful and offers it to me, and it tastes like heaven.

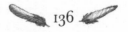

Marley grins. 'So this is it. Our breakthrough moment. The gig that will take us from promising new band to rich and famous!'

'Like we haven't heard that one before,' George groans.

'Huh?' Bex says. 'What breakthrough gig?'

'We're only headlining a major gig in Birmingham city centre,' he crows. 'A paid gig too. There'll be TV and newspaper coverage and we can invite Ked Wilder . . . fingers crossed he'll come!'

I feel like someone has poured ice water down my back. I'm cold all over, shocked, shaken.

'What?' I ask quietly. 'When? What kind of gig?'

'The council's putting on a big party for the Christmas lights switch-on, on the first of December,' he says. 'They want to showcase Midlands talent, with us headlining. It'll be like a festival in a city setting, with a Christmas flavour, obviously. It's tailor-made for us!'

'But – December the first is only two weeks away!' I argue, the tremor in my voice building to anger. 'I can't do it!'

'Sure you can,' Marley says. 'D'you think we'd have got you on board if we didn't think you could do this? We're

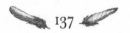

all behind you, Phoenix. You're pushing us up a notch, taking us out of our comfort zone . . .'

Marley's words are like petrol on a bonfire, and my anger flares. 'What about *my* comfort zone?' I snap. 'I haven't sung in public since I was ten years old. This was not what we agreed. You said I'd have time to get used to it all, time to perfect things. I can't do this. I won't!'

'It's jumping in at the deep end, sure,' he insists. 'But you're hardly the shy, retiring type, are you?'

'How would you even know, Marley?' I snap. 'You met me, what, all of a fortnight ago, and I've only been in the band for ten days of that. I can't do this!'

'It's not just about Phoenix, either,' Bex chips in. 'The whole dynamic of the band has changed, and we're still getting used to that! The gig sounds great, but the timing is all wrong. We'll have to turn it down.'

Marley rolls his eyes. 'We won't get a better opportunity,' he argues. 'They want us, they've asked us specially . . . and I've agreed. Let's get on with making sure it's a smash, OK?'

There's an awkward silence, and I feel fear and dismay crashing through my body like an avalanche, extinguishing my dreams. For a little while I'd let myself think I could do this, but the fantasy was never going to last.

'You agreed?' I say calmly into the quiet. '*You* agreed, Marley? I thought we were a team? You had no right to make that decision on our behalf!'

'We can't possibly be ready in two weeks!' Lee says, backing me up.

'No way,' Lexie agrees.

'Why can't you guys trust me?' Marley says, exasperated. 'I only want what's best for the band, you know that! The promoter contacted me during half-term week, and I followed it up because it was a total no-brainer – great publicity, a huge audience and an eye-watering fee on top of it all. And then we lost Sasha, and I panicked, but there was no need because we *can* do this!'

Lexie looks upset. 'But, Marley, that's not the point. We're a team – we make decisions together . . . and you've been hiding all this stuff from us for weeks! If you'd told us earlier, maybe we'd have agreed to give it a go –'

'I wouldn't have,' I snap. 'No way!'

'You see?' Marley argues. 'You'd have said it was impossible, but look how far we've come in ten days! You're

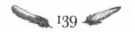

a natural, Phoenix, and yes, OK, we've had to change things around a little, adapt, but we're almost there, I promise!'

'Not sure we are,' George sulks. 'You've jazzed up the melodies, put in a load of new stuff. There's more input now for Happi, Romy, Dylan and Bex . . . but less for me and Sami. There's hardly any flute or cello now. Maybe it's not rock and roll enough?'

Sami looks up from his sketchbook. 'But we're not rock and roll anyway!' he argues. 'Or we didn't used to be. I am not sure what we are now . . .'

The words slice into me like razor blades. I try hard not to take them personally, but they still add up to one thing – the band has changed now that I'm in it, and not everyone is happy about that. I take the hurt and turn it into anger, the way I always do.

'Fine,' I say. 'I didn't ask to join your band in the first place, but you nagged me into it then changed all the rules, and now it's my fault things have changed? I never asked for this, not any of it, and I won't miss it either!'

Even as I say it, I know it's not true. In just ten days the Lost & Found has become the most important thing in my life, and I don't want to lose it.

I'm writing it down because you don't seem
to believe it when I say it out loud, or when
Marley says it. But you need to believe it, OK?

You.

Are.

Something.

Special.

Lee x+

13

Something Special

Everyone is talking at once, telling me that Marley's an idiot, that I can't leave, that things can be sorted.

'The band needs you, Phoenix,' Lee argues. 'You're – I dunno, something special. You can't go . . . you just can't!'

Marley sighs. 'I shouldn't have sprung this on you, but I meant it when I said we'd support you, Phoenix, and we will. Lee's right . . . you're something special!'

I fight the impulse to stomp out and slam the door. Do I really want to run away from all this? The band is a long way from perfect and Marley can be a total nightmare, but I'm every bit as bad. I'm supposed to be working on my temper, keeping my cool. I dunk my chocolate flake with trembling fingers and try to act like I don't care. I'm not fooling anybody, not even myself.

I notice Lee scribbling on a scrap of paper with a worn-down pencil from his pocket, watch him fold it up, smaller and smaller. He passes me the note underneath the table, and I open it out, read the message, smile.

'I may be an idiot, but you can't say I'm not doing my best for the band,' Marley argues. 'I could have said no to the gig, but why let a chance like this go when I know we can do it? Is it bad timing? Sure. Will it be hard work? Yes, of course . . . but you lot can do it. You always put a hundred per cent in, no matter what. OK, we'll have to practise pretty much every day, but we've done that before . . . and I swear it will be worth it!'

'You said they invited us back in October,' George points out. 'Won't they be expecting the old version of the Lost & Found?'

Marley sighs. 'Things are changing, but you can see how cool it's going to be. The festival will love it and so will our fans!'

As if to prove Marley's point, two girls approach the table. They've been sitting at a corner table with their mum, eating ice-cream sundaes and casting curious looks in our direction, and now at last they've plucked up the courage to come over. One is clutching a notebook and pen, and both look like they might explode at any moment.

'You're them, aren't you?' the smallest girl says. 'That band. The Lost & Found! We're your biggest fans! Someone at school said you split up, but it can't be true, because you're here . . . you're really here!'

'We definitely haven't split up,' Marley says with a grin. 'We've had a change of lead singer, that's all!'

The girls giggle and squeal and beg for selfies and autographs, and we all spend a few minutes signing the notebook and posing for selfies.

'Why not come and see our next gig?' Marley says.

'We will,' the girls chorus. 'When is it?'

Marley shrugs. 'Well, it was going to be the first of December at the big Christmas lights festival in Birmingham,' he says. 'But I think we might have to cancel that, and I don't know when we'll get another chance to play. I'm really sorry – the rest of the band don't want to do it.'

'Blackmail, Marley,' Bex says icily, but the girls are already dissolving into outraged squeals.

'Oh no!' they wail. 'Please do it! You're our favourite band! We'll bring all our friends! Please?'

'Oh, for goodness' sake,' Bex huffs. 'Do what you want, Marley! You probably will anyway!'

One by one, the band members turn and look at me. I hold the future of the Lost & Found in my hands, it seems, and nobody cares that I've never sung on an actual stage in my entire life before. I can't decide whether to laugh or cry.

'Your call,' Lexie adds. 'If you want to give it a shot, we'll go with it . . . but don't let Marley bully you!'

I make the mistake of looking at the two little girls again. One of them has tears in her eyes. Exasperated, I cave in. 'OK, OK, I'll do it . . .'

The girls throw their arms round me. Marley says he'll sort them out with a backstage pass each, and finally their mum comes over to usher her daughters back to the table, but by then I am pretty sure my cheeks are as red as my hair.

'Are you OK with this?' Lee asks.

145

'No, not really!'

'You'll be amazing,' Marley insists. 'We're a team. We'll make every single song the best it can be, and Jake will make sure the tech is perfect and Sasha will do the make-up and styling and it'll be epic, I know it will. Thanks, Phoenix, seriously. I know this is a leap of faith –'

'Without a safety net!' I remind him.

'You won't need one,' he promises. 'You really won't.'

I barely notice Marley nudging Lexie, but then I see Happi and Romy opening their violin cases, Sami taking out his flute, George opening the cello case. I'm supposed to be the singer, but it's Lexie, Romy and Happi who start to sing, launching into the song Marley created from my 'Fireworks' poem while the others are on their feet, tuning in with their instruments. Dylan, without a drum kit, is bashing out the beat on the tabletop with two of the wooden spoons that show the table numbers.

'C'mon, Phoenix,' Lee says with a grin. 'This is the smaller gig you wanted, right?'

In the corner the two little girls are wide-eyed and suddenly the whole cafe is silent, watching, waiting. I get to my feet, my mouth somehow finding the words. We've practised so much they're engraved on my memory, stamped on my soul, and I forget I'm in a crowded cafe surrounded by strangers and lose myself in the song. I stamp my feet and whirl around and when Lee adds a little dance to his trumpet solo I mirror his steps without even trying. Even Lexie, Romy and Happi are swaying with the music.

People are taking photos and videos on their phones, but this doesn't bother me at all. If anything, it spurs me on. When I get to the last verse, I dance right up to the two little girls and pull them to their feet, bringing them into the middle of it all, making it something special.

Marley is grinning his approval, and Bex laughs as she strums her bass, and I'm on such a high by the time we're done that I barely register the shouts and applause.

That night, I add Lee's crumpled note to the Quality Street tin. Marley is right. Something very special is happening here, and I can't quite believe I'm part of it. Something special could happen between me and Lee, too . . . if I am brave enough to let it. I fit the lid back on the Quality Street tin, smiling.

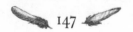

Dear Phoenix,

I trust you are settling in well with your grandmother. I have arranged to send her an allowance to cover your board and lodging, with a small amount left over so you have some pocket money. Do your best not to be a nuisance. I'm sure you will take the local school in your stride – you are a very clever girl, for all your faults. Do not let me down.

You will be pleased to hear that the insurance have agreed to pay out on the fire damage, so the dorm will get a new roof and be as good as new once everything is done.

In haste,
Vivi Winter

14

Countdown

My mother does not believe in FaceTime or phone calls or social media, not unless they're something to do with work. No, she gets out her fountain pen and her fancy watermarked paper and writes me a letter, and she doesn't even sign it with a kiss. There is no mention of missing me, but what's new?

Anyhow, the letter must mean that she cares, at least a little bit. She has failed to mould me into a carbon copy of herself, an acceptable daughter. From the moment I started to show a streak of rebelliousness, a longing to run wild, climb trees, argue back, the message has been loud and clear – I am not the kind of daughter Mum was hoping for. She has written me off as a hopeless case, a truant, a troublemaker . . . but maybe I can still make her proud? Maybe.

I might send her an email and tell her about the gig, anyhow.

I look at the calendar in the kitchen and cross off another day. Eight days until the Christmas lights switch on . . . and, in spite of the gorgeous coffee shop mini gig and the flurry of Instagram pictures and posts that followed, I still have a sick, sour feeling in my belly when I think about it. The event has been advertised in the local paper – a reporter came along to the old railway carriage and took some photos and asked questions, and yesterday there was a feature about our new line-up and how 'the band's new lead singer, flame-haired teen Phoenix Marlow, delighted two young fans by singing specially for them in the Leaping Llama'.

Cringe.

The last time I passed Matt Brennan at school, he snarled at me and called me something very rude, so I called him something even ruder back. I think he is furious that he missed out on the latest Lost & Found 'scoop'.

As for Marley, he's clipped out the newspaper piece and sent it to Ked Wilder, along with an invitation to come and watch the show. I thought he was joking but Bex and Lexie insist he's not. Apparently Ked is a big fan of the Lost & Found and was keen to help them record their first EP, before Sasha got ill and the whole project fell to bits. He even had plans to get the band on the *Lola Rockett Show*, which is hands down the coolest TV music show ever, but that didn't happen, of course.

Getting Ked back on side would be a real achievement.

I mention it to Grandma Lou and she says that if he does come he can stay here, because they're best friends and never miss a chance to catch up. It's not that I am mad about his music or anything, but I can't help being impressed because Ked Wilder is properly famous, and who wouldn't want to meet a sixties pop legend? Maybe he can give me some tips on how not to feel sick about performing on stage.

I am definitely getting on top of the playlist now. With daily rehearsals and a healthy dose of terror about what might happen if I mess up, the songs are sounding slick and strong, and the band are pitch perfect on the accompaniments Marley has drawn up for them. The sound is loud and sassy and dancier than before, a crazy mix of stroppy and joyful. I love it.

'It sounds so different when you sing it,' Lexie says at practice, later that day. 'Different, but good! Like you've turned it inside out and dipped it in darkness and magic!'

'Thank you, I think!'

'Something special,' Lee reminds me, reunited once more with his battered trilby – I found it in the old oak tree and staged a rescue, but the hat is even more bedraggled than before. Lee doesn't seem to mind, though, and I like him for that. One day, when I'm old and grey and all this Lost & Found stuff is over and Lee is just a distant memory, I'll be able to look through the old Quality Street tin with all my treasures – the diaries, the lists, the poems, the pictures, the letters from Mum and the note from Lee . . . the little pieces of my past. It will always make me smile.

'Was I right about this, or was I right?' Marley crows as another song pulls to a close. 'We are *so* ready for this gig. This is the best we've ever been, and we still have a week to polish and perfect things. The gig is going to be epic!'

'If we don't all die of exhaustion first,' Bex grumbles. 'You're pushing us too hard. I've got GCSE mocks to revise for, y'know . . . There's more to life than music!'

'Not much more,' Marley says with a grin. 'Things happen fast in this industry, and we can't afford to waste a minute. Now we're back on track again, we might be able to pick things up again with Ked Wilder and get that EP out before Christmas. Maybe we can still get on to the *Lola Rockett Show.*'

Lee shakes his head. 'Marley, man, that's not gonna happen! Be realistic!'

'Being realistic won't get us anywhere,' Marley declares. 'I'm telling you, if we get on Lola Rockett's New Year show we're made. It's a ticket to stardom!'

'But we don't have a record deal or an EP yet,' I argue. 'Let's not run before we can walk!'

'Phoenix, Phoenix, wake up and smell the coffee!' Marley says. 'We are not going to get anywhere taking baby steps. We have to run – not just run, we have to sprint as if our lives depend on it! This is a race to the top, and Lola Rockett can help us get there!'

Bex rolls her eyes. 'You're on a whole different planet to the rest of us, Marley. Get real!'

'Where's the fun in that?' he counters. 'Listen – changing the subject – I think we should cover a Christmas song as our finale at the festival . . . The crowd would love it!'

'They would,' Lee admits grudgingly. We debate for a while about the best song before settling on an old-timey classic called 'Let it Snow'. Marley has already messed about with the tune and the tempo, giving it a fresh feel and showcasing the violins, cello, flute and trumpet. I have a go at singing it with the others doing their best to support, and even in that ragged state it sounds pretty awesome.

'Marley is a full-on megalomaniac with slave-driver tendencies and zero people skills,' Lee tells me under his breath. 'He does care, though, and his instincts are good most of the time.'

'I guess he's OK as tyrants go,' I say.

Six days before the gig, Sasha comes to the old railway carriage after rehearsal to show us her styling ideas. She has two main looks – one with the whole band dressed in outsize red sweaters with black skinny jeans or leggings, and the other based on magpie chic, with everyone in ragged blue-black costumes, twigs and feathers in their hair.

'The first look would be cheap to do . . . I can get charity-shop jumpers, and as this is an outdoor event in December, it might be the best choice.'

I run a finger lightly across the magpie drawings. 'These, though . . . they're amazing!' I say. 'Just stunning, Sasha . . . You're so talented!'

She looks pleased at the compliment. 'I got the idea from Pie, obviously,' she says. 'He's so cool! I know he can't come to actual gigs with you, so I was thinking of ways to keep that same kind of vibe . . .'

Pie, bored with perching on my shoulder to inspect the designs, flutters off to patrol the countertop in search of biscuit crumbs. When I look over he is gazing at his own reflection in a shiny silver spoon . . . he really is the vainest magpie ever.

'Why can't Pie come to gigs?' I question. 'He doesn't mind loud music – he's used to everyone in the band now . . .'

'You'd bring him to gigs?' Marley echoes. 'Wow! That'd really set us apart from the crowd!'

'He's my lucky charm,' I explain. 'He makes me feel more confident, that's all.'

'In that case he's coming to every performance,' Marley says. 'On the plus side, he already has a magpie costume . . .'

'If we do use this idea, I'd do blue-green iridescent make-up to go with it . . . and paint feathers on your hands and arms. It'd look amazing with your flame-red hair, Phoenix!'

'It would,' Marley agrees. 'But no way could you make all the costumes in six days. Just getting the feathers would be a nightmare. Let's save the magpie theme for whatever comes next . . .'

'Sure,' Sasha says. 'The jumpers will be way easier to sort. I'm going to do everything I can to help the band get their breakthrough moment, Marley, even though I'm not on stage any more.'

'I know, Sash,' Marley says. 'We hated to lose you, but look at how you've been these last few weeks – like a weight's been lifted from your shoulders. And you'll always be a part of the Lost & Found – without you we wouldn't have a proper look, we'd just be a bunch of teenagers in random clothes . . .'

Sasha beams. 'Thanks, Marley. I've already found a gorgeous moss-green mohair jumper for you, Phoenix. It'll single you out as the lead singer and it'll look incredible with your hair . . .'

'Cool,' I say, and try to ignore the churning in my belly.

Two days before the gig, Grandma Lou tells me that Ked Wilder will indeed be coming, and he will indeed be staying at Greystones. I pass this information on to Marley in the school lunch hall.

'I knew it!' he yells. 'I totally knew it! Didn't I tell you? Didn't I say he'd come? Didn't I say you should trust me?'

'Once or twice,' Bex grumbles.

'Well, I was right, wasn't I? This is it. Ked really believes in us, and this time we're going to nail it!'

No pressure, then.

'I hope you're right, Marley,' George says with a sigh. 'Things have changed a lot since Ked last saw us play . . .'

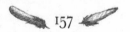

157

'In a good way, though,' Marley argues. 'We've stepped up a level since Phoenix joined, I keep telling you!'

George looks gloomy, but he holds Marley's gaze. 'Yeah, you keep telling us,' he says, and he pushes his chair back and picks up his rucksack and walks away, leaving a plate of untouched curry and rice on the table.

'OK,' Marley says. 'He's not happy, is he?'

'I'll talk to him,' Sami says. 'I understand . . . not so much cello, not so much flute. Things change. Whatever!' He shoulders his bag and hurries after George.

'OK, so there's less flute and cello in the new arrangements,' Marley says, exasperated. 'So what? We're a pop band, not an orchestra! We have to think about what our fans want!'

'Maybe our fans like flute and cello?' Lexie says. 'I know I do. And maybe George and Sami are tired, too, Marley – you've been pushing us all to the max. Anyone else here remember when being in a band used to be fun?'

Lexie shoves her plate away and follows George and Sami.

'That I did not expect,' Marley says, biting into his toasted cheese sandwich. 'They're dropping like flies.

Better see if I can talk them round.' He saunters off to make the peace, but I'm panicking. A small rebellion seems to be brewing because things have changed, and things have changed because of me.

'Is this my fault?' I say in a very small voice.

'No,' Bex argues. 'If anything, it's Marley's for making things happen too fast and putting us under so much pressure. He has no patience – he wants fame, fortune and mass adulation, preferably by tomorrow.'

'My brother's a megalomaniac,' Dylan agrees. 'Fact.'

'It'll be OK,' Happi promises. 'Things always get a bit stressy when we have a big gig looming – it's happened before and it'll happen again. Nobody's fault.'

But it feels like mine.

To: schoolprincipal@bellvaleladiescollege.org

Subject: Hello

Hi Mum,

Thanks for your letter. I have settled in really well and the schoolwork is fine. I don't think you will have noticed, but I brought Pie with me and he is loving life now that there is no cat to stalk him and no groundsman taking pot shots at him with an air rifle.

This may surprise you but I have joined a band called the Lost & Found. We have a big gig scheduled for 1st December. It's a sort of winter festival, and we are headlining. If you want to come, I know Grandma Lou would be happy to see you. Of course, this is very short notice and you probably have work and everything.

Phoenix

Send

15

The Point of No Return

Mum doesn't come, of course. I didn't think she would, but even so I let myself hope, just a little bit. This morning's email reply, a terse three lines, dismisses my request as far too late and far too silly. I feel like an irritating kid clamouring for her mum's attention all over again . . . It's a place I've been so many times before.

I delete the email and tilt my chin up, determined not to let the hurt show.

I didn't learn to ride a bike until I was ten years old, the summer before I started at Bellvale. Mum had been promoted to school principal and we'd moved out of the village into a small cottage on the Bellvale grounds. That six weeks was the only time I spent there, really . . . after that, I moved into the dorm and the game of pretending that Vivi Winter was not my mother began.

That first summer, though, we were the only people at Bellvale, apart from a few workmen painting classrooms and plastering walls. Mum was busy with her conquering-the-world plans, so I roamed all over the grounds, climbed the hills, prowled through the woods. I found an unlocked bicycle in one of the storerooms and taught myself to ride, and after a few circuits of the drive I wheeled it up to the top of a hill and pushed off.

When you're freewheeling you start slowly, wobbling, and then you pass the point of no return and the wheels are spinning and the bike clatters over potholes and stones, shaking your bones so hard it's a miracle you don't fall off into the nearest ditch – but you don't, you hang on. You hang on for dear life with the wind in your hair and your heart in your mouth and it feels like flying, like freedom. You open your mouth and yell as loud as you possibly can, maybe with terror, maybe with pure joy, most likely with both mixed up together.

That night I went back to the cottage with cuts and bruises all over my arms and legs, and some spectacular scratches on my face from where I'd fallen off into a patch of brambles. Mum forbade me from riding again and put a padlock on the storeroom door, and after that I had to get my kicks from winding up teachers, playing practical jokes and burning down the school. Well, not quite, but you get the picture.

The day of the great Christmas light switch-on is the closest I have ever been since then to that freewheeling feeling. I'm at the top of the hill and I know it's going to be a bumpy ride, but still, there's no turning back.

The last two days have been crazy. There've been costume fittings, pep talks, last-minute tweaks to the playlist. Yesterday we had two rehearsals in one day, and there is still a storm cloud of resentment hovering around George that threatens to descend at any moment.

'It's band life,' Bex tells me carelessly. 'You'll get used to it.'

'What if I don't?' I ask. 'What if I can't do this?'

'You can totally do it,' she says. 'Wait and see!'

Marley and I go to tell Mr Simpson about the gig and ask if the band can take the afternoon off school. Typically he refuses. 'You're not exactly model pupils, are you?' he grumbles. 'Why should I give you time off?'

Marley threatens to call his contact at Birmingham council, and Mr Simpson caves in, admitting that our headliner gig will reflect well on the school. We catch the train to Birmingham after lunch, with Pie in the cat basket. Jake's stepdad, Sheddie, took our equipment over earlier, and it has already been unpacked by the festival crew.

We've seen the Green Room, a Portakabin with bench seating, mirrors and a loo. It's not posh, but the mirrors do have light bulbs all round them, like you see in the movies, and there's a kettle and a seemingly endless supply of hot chocolate, cola, biscuits, fruit and sandwiches. Not that I can actually eat – I don't have butterflies in my tummy so much as a herd of dancing elephants.

I duck out of the Portakabin with Pie to look around. Pie is wary of the city noises and hides under my hair, digging his claws into my shoulder a little more firmly than usual. '*Crak, crak, craaak,*' he squawks, stretching his wings and causing a minor stir with passers-by.

I keep walking, partly to calm Pie down and partly because there is so much to see. A big festival-style stage takes pride of place in the centre of the shopping area, and men and women in hi-vis jackets move purposefully around the site doing last-minute jobs: checking safety barriers, taping down wires, testing amps and lights. Beyond the festival enclosure, stalls have appeared ready to sell hot food and drinks, and half a dozen TV vans are parked up with cameras and sound equipment being moved into place.

Above it all hang intricate cobwebs of Christmas lights, strung high across the wide shopping street. Final touches and tweaks are being made by a technician in a hard hat working from a cherry picker, and a couple of tattooed guys are testing out a laser light show from their vantage point at the mixing desk. Jake has appointed himself as work experience, running errands and fetching coffees for them.

Lee appears from a nearby shop doorway, swigging Coke and falling into step beside me. 'Amazing, isn't it?' he says. 'How's Pie? Not freaking out?'

'Not sure he likes it, but he's OK,' I say. 'I hope he copes on stage . . . He loves rehearsals, but this is something different. For both of us. If Pie freaks, I'll put him in his cat basket and Sasha can look after him backstage . . .'

'What if you freak?' Lee teases. 'Do we have a cat basket for you?'

'I'll be fine,' I insist, sounding more confident than I feel. 'I'm really stoked to be here . . . I've worked hard, I know what I'm doing, and this is my chance to prove it!'

Lee gives me the side-eye.

'OK, OK, I'm terrified,' I admit. 'I didn't sleep last night, running through all the things that could go wrong . . .'

'Like what?'

'Like forgetting the words,' I tell him. 'Or singing out of tune. Or tripping over my own feet when I'm dancing, or getting tangled up in a trailing wire and electrocuting myself as I fall off the stage into the audience –'

'Stop right there,' he says. 'None of that is going to happen. You know the songs inside out, you couldn't sing out of tune if you tried, your dancing is super-cute and there are no trailing wires and nothing that can electrocute you. And if you fall off the stage, I'll jump right after you and everyone will think it's part of the show . . .'

Pie hops across to Lee's shoulder and he puts a hand up to hang on to his hat, laughing. 'Just don't think about the cameras and the film crews,' he tells me with a grin. 'Or Ked Wilder, or how Marley will strangle us if that elusive EP deal doesn't happen. Think about those little girls from the Leaping Llama, and how much they love you. OK?'

'OK!'

My mobile buzzes. Sasha wants us back at the Portakabin Green Room for make-up and costume, and this time when we head inside the place is hectic. Marley and Dylan are leaning in to the light-bulb mirrors trying to see who can perfect the most artfully tousled hair, and George is refusing to wear his red charity-shop jumper because it has a reindeer on it.

'Look in the suitcase, George,' Sasha says, exasperated, as she delicately outlines a snowflake on Romy's cheek with face paints. 'There might be a spare one. But it looks fine, it really does . . .'

'I don't like dressing up,' George grumbles. 'It's not what I joined a band for!'

Marley silently rolls his eyes and Sasha chucks me a carrier bag of stuff and tells me to get ready, so I duck into the toilet cubicle and change. The green mohair jumper Sasha has picked out for me is a beautiful jewel-bright colour, but it's huge . . . the wide neckline slides off one shoulder, and the whole thing hangs down almost to my knees. I consider trading it for George's reindeer jumper, but then I spot a studded belt lurking at the bottom of the bag. With the belt slung round my hips, the jumper transforms into a fluffy minidress, half punk and half sixties chic.

In the very bottom of the bag there is a flat box, the size of an exercise book. I take the lid off carefully to find a beautiful ear cuff fashioned from silver wire with magpie feathers fanned out along the curve. I push my hair back on one side and fit the cuff round the back of my ear. It feels heavy and cool against my skin, and the feathers press against my hair like a blue-black sunburst. Sasha has made me something inspired by her magpie sketches and it is absolutely beautiful.

Pie obviously agrees, because he swoops back on to my shoulder the moment I emerge, and the rest of the band give me the thumbs-up as Sasha ushers me into the make-up chair. 'I love it, Sasha,' I say. 'The ear thing, whatever you call it . . . it's awesome! Thank you so much!'

'You're going to be brilliant,' she tells me, and I lean back and close my eyes as she gets to work. Ten minutes later I open my eyes and see someone I hardly recognize gazing back at me from the mirror. She is fierce and striking and dramatic, her green eyes lined with black, a delicate snowflake painted on one cheek, a prancing magpie patrolling the back of her chair. Blazing auburn and cerise hair falls in spiral curls from behind a feathered earpiece and her mouth moves slowly from a perfect 'O' of surprise to the widest grin. The main thing I notice about the girl in the mirror is that she looks bright and brave and beautiful, and for once in my life the way I feel inside matches up.

The door opens and a girl with headphones and a clipboard appears. 'Five minutes to soundcheck!' she yells. 'All bands on stage and ready to go!'

Time folds in on itself. One moment we're watching the other bands soundcheck – there's a teen boy band from Birmingham and a hip-hop combo performing before

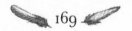

us – and the next we've soundchecked too, scoping out our places on the stage, adjusting the mics, playing one song three times over until the sound guys have the mix right. And then the light is fading around us and people are filing into the enclosure and someone introduces us to the Lord Mayor. Someone else introduces us to the presenter, a bouncy bloke from a kids' TV programme, and a young woman with ten piercings in one ear interviews us for a music blog.

Finally a spotlight appears on stage and the bouncy TV guy gallops into the centre of it and gets the crowd cheering and whooping as he introduces the boy band. They play twenty minutes of cheesy Christmas covers, and suddenly I'm worrying that the crowd will hate us because they won't know the words to our songs and they won't like the way I sing, and someone will probably report me to the RSPCA for having a magpie on my shoulder. The hip-hop group are next, and they're totally different . . . original songs and lots of energetic dancing, even if they are a bit clichéd with their backwards baseball caps and low-slung baggy jeans. The crowd love them too, and the tiniest spark of hope ignites inside me that perhaps the crowd will like whatever is put in front of them, because they're here and they're hyped and they're happy, and they really only want to see the big lights switch on anyway.

'Break a leg,' Bex whispers as the hip-hop kids finish and the presenter starts telling the crowd that the Lost & Found are the best-kept secret on the Midlands music scene. 'I mean, not literally, but y'know!'

'You'll smash it,' Marley promises, and I instantly think of my fears of falling offstage and picture myself being stretchered away with two broken legs.

'Think of those two little girls,' Lee says, and he takes my hand and we walk together on to the stage, and the crowd is going wild. Pie, his claws digging into my shoulder, gives a euphoric squawk, and Lee lets go of my hand and steps back into his place, but I don't think I can even breathe, let alone sing. I am dazzled by camera flashes, lights, by the sheer size of the crowd below. My body is full of adrenaline and flames and fear, and just for a moment I falter.

Marley grabs his mic.

'Hello, Birmingham!' he yells, and there's an answering roar of applause. 'We're the Lost & Found and we're

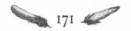

thrilled to be here with you tonight! This first song's a new one – it's called "Fireworks"!'

It's my top-of-the-hill moment.

The band crash in with the opening chords and I step up to the mic, and suddenly I am past the point of no return. I am freewheeling, euphoric, singing my heart out, the beat of the music pulsing through my veins like blood. There is no better feeling in the world.

MILLFORD TEEN BAND THE LOST & FOUND

headlined a successful outdoor concert of new musical talent on the afternoon of 1 December, as part of the Birmingham Big Christmas Lights Switch-On. The band, who have recently had a change of lead singer, with fourteen-year-old Phoenix Marlow now taking centre stage, wowed the audience with a set of original tracks before finishing with a cover of the much-loved classic 'Let It Snow', during which two delighted young fans were invited onstage to join the band. Phoenix, who performed with her pet magpie perched on her shoulder throughout, has a voice of such pure beauty, energy, attitude and charm that it seems certain you will be hearing more of her before long.

16

Ked Wilder

Afterwards I was so high from it all that I barely remember anything. I felt like I was wired to the National Grid and fizzing with electricity. I remember the cheers of the crowd, and I remember spotting the little girls from the Leaping Llama at the front of the crowd and asking them up to sing with us. Marley keeps saying this was a stroke of genius, but at the time it just felt like the right thing to do.

My memory of the actual light switch-on itself is hazy, but it was done by Ked Wilder, who turned up with his famous friend Lola Rockett. Marley nearly wet himself when he realized she was in the audience, I swear.

'I told you, I told you, I told you!' he crows later.

We talk for a while with Ked and Lola and Grandma Lou, squashed into a circle of vintage armchairs arranged round a carefully tended firepit, next to a stall selling mulled wine and spiced fruit juice. This is my first glimpse of Ked – a tall, stringy guy dressed all in black with a jaunty fedora tilted back over his grey moptop hair. His eyes are hidden behind mirrored shades even though it's a cold, dark night in December. He looks like a cartoon of himself, but he smiles a lot, and it's impossible not to warm to him.

Lola Rockett, of course, is exactly the way she looks on TV . . . small, frantic, ridiculously pretty, and determined to be everybody's new best friend.

'Ked's told me so much about you,' she says, leaning in to focus on me and Marley. 'He's been singing your praises for months now, but with losing your old lead singer . . . well, we all assumed things would fall apart. When Ked asked me to come along tonight I'll admit I thought it would be a waste of time. I only agreed because my sister lives in Birmingham and it's a chance to see her . . .'

Ked laughs. 'Let's just say it hasn't been a waste of time,' he says. 'Far from it!'

'I know!' Lola Rockett squeals. 'I'm amazed! I'm astonished! I'm beyond impressed! And you're all so young!'

'With a lead singer who's been on board for less than a month,' Ked adds. 'Extraordinary!'

Lola Rockett turns her shrewd blue eyes on me. 'Extraordinary indeed,' she says. 'Everything about you – the eyes, the hair, the feathers, this amazing creature . . .' She stretches a long index finger towards Pie, who hops away, alarmed, on to the safety of Lee's shoulder.

The turquoise-tipped finger lifts a hank of my dip-dyed auburn hair and pokes at the magpie feathers adorning my lovely ear cuff. I feel like a butterfly pinned to a board, being examined with a magnifying glass.

'Wonderful, wonderful,' Lola marvels. 'Quite unique! And what a story! My viewers would absolutely love you, Phoenix. Well, all of you, obviously. We'll definitely have to get you on the show. I'll get my people to call your people!'

Marley's face is bright with hope. 'The New Year show?' he asks. 'That would be amazing!'

Lola Rockett laughs. 'The New Year show? Oh, no, no, not that. We've been booked up since October! I'm sorry,

these things are organized so far in advance. It's all tied up with the record companies and the promoters, and, well, you don't actually have a deal yet, or an EP . . .'

'It's only a matter of time,' Ked says kindly, but Marley looks devastated, as if Lola Rockett has stomped all over his hopes and dreams with her turquoise-leather stiletto boots, as if all the hard work has been for nothing.

Bex puts her arms round him, hugs him tight and tells him not to be such an idiot, and I feel a bit sorry for him too. I can see that for all his slave-driver tendencies and wild ambitions, Marley is just a music-mad kid with a talent for making catchy tunes and dreams of fame and fortune. You can't really blame him for that.

The evening flies past in a blur. We are interviewed by four different newspapers, two radio stations and the local BBC news programme. Everybody asks about Pie, and I have to explain over and over how I rescued him as a chick and raised him by hand and how, even though I released him back into the wild, he kept coming back. I don't mention the bit about smuggling him down from the Scottish highlands in a cat basket . . . do you blame me?

We chat a bit to the other bands too, and the girl backing singer/dancer from the hip-hop group (I think they're called Pretty Street) tells me she used to play keyboards in the Lost & Found. Bobbi-Jo, her name is. 'You've got great stage presence,' she tells me. 'I liked being part of the Lost & Found, but it wasn't really the right fit for me. I'm happier with the hip-hop lads!'

In between, we sign hundreds of autographs and pose for loads of selfies. Everyone wants a picture with Pie.

'Fame at last,' Lee says, and I laugh and tell him I can't take it in, and he says I'd better get used to it.

It's past ten by the time we get back to Greystones. Lola Rockett has gone off to stay with her sister so it's just Ked and Grandma Lou and me, sitting in the kitchen drinking hot chocolate. Kind of surreal, but there you go.

'When Marley told me he'd found an amazing new lead singer, I did not expect it would be Louisa's granddaughter,' Ked is saying. 'What are the chances? I'm totally blown away – you have the most incredible voice, Phoenix!'

'That's not what my mum used to say . . .'

 178

Ked laughs. 'I remember your mother as a little girl,' he tells me. 'She was always very serious. And not the best of judges when it comes to music, it seems!'

'Not at all,' Grandma Lou says.

'You're more like your grandmother,' Ked says with a sigh. 'In looks and perhaps in spirit too. I'm very curious, though . . . where does the musical streak come from? Your father? His family, perhaps?'

'He's an accountant,' I explain. 'I don't think I've inherited any musical genes at all . . . it must be purely random.'

'And then there's Pie,' he goes on. 'He's a very handsome bird, and an important addition to the band. I'm really glad I took the time to come up and see you play!'

'I'm glad, too,' I say, stifling a yawn.

Ked smiles, and I have the strangest feeling that I've met him somewhere before, even though I obviously never have. I think he just has that kind of face . . . and that kind of personality, the kind that draws people in, makes you feel you've known them forever.

'You have a huge talent, from what I've seen,' he says. 'I think you have a bright future ahead – in fact, I know

you do, Phoenix. A very unusual name, too . . . I have a song called "Phoenix"!'

'Yes, I love it! When I was small I loved that there was a song with my name in, and the girl in the song is so wild and free, too!'

Ked beams. 'Remember, Louisa?' he says.

'Of course I do!'

I don't ask what it was that Grandma Lou remembers. I don't ask anything, because now that the buzz of the gig had finally begun to wear off, exhaustion has wrapped itself round me like a warm, soft blanket.

Ked reaches out and takes Grandma Lou's hand in his own, smiling. It seems a bit weird, with them being so old and stuff, but Grandma Lou has already explained that Ked is her best and oldest friend. They met long ago in the sixties when she was a young model and he was an up-and-coming pop star, and although their love affair lasted only a year or so, their friendship weathered every storm, becoming stronger with the passing of time. I try to imagine them young and in love, but I'm just too tired to do it.

I say goodnight and take my hot chocolate up to bed.

*

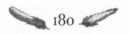

Next day, I sleep late and Ked is long gone, heading back to his home in Devon, by the time I surface.

'He's so cool,' I tell Grandma Lou. 'With his mirrored shades and his funny hat and winkle-picker shoes . . . and his fancy famous friends too. That includes you, by the way!'

'Why thank you!' She laughs, dropping a jokey curtsey before dunking a chocolate chip cookie into her lapsang tea.

'But he's really nice, too,' I continue. 'Down to earth and funny and . . . well, you know, kind. I really liked him.'

Grandma Lou's eyes mist over. 'Oh, I'm so very glad about that, Phoenix!'

'Shame about Lola Rockett's New Year show,' I comment. 'Marley'd set his heart on that. But she says she'll invite us on sometime, so that's almost as good. And the gig was . . . just awesome, Grandma Lou. I was so scared beforehand. I didn't think I could do it. But I did do it, and I loved it! I really, really loved it!'

'Everybody else loved it, too,' Grandma Lou says. 'I was so proud!'

I don't waste time wondering if Mum would have been proud too. I already know the answer to that.

PHOENIX MARLOW, fourteen-year-old lead singer of tipped-for-the-top teen band the **Lost & Found**, made a memorable debut last night at Birmingham's Big Christmas Lights Switch-On, and it wasn't just the pet magpie who performed with her who was a hit. Pure and powerful vocals, a stunning set list of original songs and a commanding stage presence instantly earned Phoenix a legion of new fans. We can see a very bright future for Phoenix – and for the **Lost & Found**.

17

Christmas is Coming

'Nothing like this has ever happened before,' Bex marvels. 'A full-page spread on the band, two half-page features, a three-quarter-page one and a colour spread!'

'Did you see the BBC local news round-up?' Lexie adds. 'Three whole minutes ... and that gorgeous interview with Phoenix and the Leaping Llama girls!'

'Every single review is positive,' Marley concludes. 'Phoenix, you're a natural ... you know just what to say to keep those journalists lapping it up!'

'I don't even remember what I said,' I admit. 'I was on such a high I couldn't think straight!'

'Well, it was perfect,' Marley says. 'All this coverage . . . and all of it saying that the Lost & Found are better than ever, that we're right on the edge of the big time! Didn't I tell you the hard work would be worth it?'

It's Monday, and newspaper articles from the last few days are spread out across the table in the school canteen for everyone to see. As well as pictures of the band, there are several close-ups of me with Pie on my shoulder, my hair flying out as I dance, lost in the music. I spent so long worrying about the song lyrics and dance steps and putting on a brave face that I didn't even think of this aspect of fronting a band – you are the one people notice.

'No date yet for that mythical EP you promised,' George grumbles. 'And no TV slot either. What's the point of being on the edge of the big time if we never get past that point?'

'We will,' Marley promises. 'It's only a matter of time. We have to stick with the daily practice, stay focused . . .'

'We can't practise every day, Marley,' Lexie says. 'Not in December. Have a heart . . . Christmas is coming!'

'Ked could call at any moment to invite us down to Devon to record that EP,' Marley argues. 'We have to be ready! What's more important?'

Nobody knows quite what to say to this. I mean, I'm the lead singer and even I think daily rehearsals might be a bit much right now, but Marley is imagining the future unfurl before him. He can't see anything but his name in lights.

'Unbelievable,' George says at last. 'Can't any of you see what's happening here?'

'George has a point,' Bex comments. 'We can't keep up this level of pressure – if you push too hard, you'll break the band! I have mock GCSEs to study for. We all have stuff on, especially in the run-up to Christmas. C'mon . . . get real, Marley!'

'You're losing the plot, Marley, mate,' Lee adds quietly.

It's hard to tell which way this is going to go.

Marley looks angry at the challenge . . . disappointed too, as if we've all let him down. And then his face breaks into a smile, and he brushes away our protests, tells us that maybe we've earned a break. Practice will be Mondays, Wednesdays, Fridays and Saturdays until such time as he hears from Ked again or gets a date to record the EP.

'We have to stay tight and strong,' he declares. 'Ready for anything. I have this feeling . . . we're so, so close. But yeah, sure . . . I guess we can slow down a bit for now. Christmas is coming!'

You can tell it's almost Christmas because the waiters in the Leaping Llama have started wearing Santa hats and even my takeaway hot chocolate – in a reusable bamboo cup – comes with a cinnamon snowflake stencilled on top.

The shops are opening late in the run-up to Christmas, and I'm out with Bex and Lexie, trying to do all our present shopping in one go. I buy a small hardback sketchbook with creamy watercolour paper for Grandma Lou in the art shop, and a red silk scarf with pale pink hearts on it for Mum in the fancy department store.

I cradle the hot chocolate in mittened hands. It's been colder these last few days, the kind of cold that means a little cloud spools out into the air in front of you when you speak, like dragon's breath.

'Can we try the charity shops, too?' Lexie suggests. 'I'm still looking for something for Sami, and I always find the best prezzies there!'

We push into the nearest one. 'You and Lee seem to be getting close,' Bex says. 'Has he asked you out yet?'

'Every other day,' I admit. 'I do like him – it's just . . . well, I don't have a very good track record when it comes to boys. Or on anything, really. I'm scared, I suppose.'

'No way,' Lexie says. 'You always seem so confident and in control . . . like you know everything about everything!'

'Ha – I know nothing at all,' I say. 'It's an act. I stick my chin in the air and make like I'm brave. It works most of the time, but I'm totally bluffing my way through, pretending I know what I'm doing!'

'Aren't we all?' Bex chips in, trying on a pink pillbox hat with a net veil. 'Anyone who says they know what they're doing is either lying or kidding themselves. It took me a long time and a lot of meltdowns to work that one out . . .'

'None of us have a clue,' Lexie says, peering out from beneath a beautiful length of green-and-gold sari fabric. 'In my experience, families aren't always the way they look in the movies . . . but there's no point dwelling on the sad bits or the bad bits. I thought I had no family left at all, but it turns out I have two lovely grandparents . . . they're friends of your gran, actually. And then there's my foster family – they're amazing, even this troublemaker here . . .' She nudges Bex.

'Hey!' Bex protests.

'So I count my blessings,' Lexie goes on. 'Look for the good stuff, Phoenix – it's always there . . .'

'Festive philosophy of the Lost & Found,' Bex says. 'She's right, though. Apart from the "troublemaker" bit. Anyway, nothing's really grabbing me here. Shall we try the place on the corner?'

In the second charity shop Bex finds an almost new veggie cookery book for her foster mum, Lexie buys a fringed woollen scarf for Sami, and I find a black wool beret in perfect condition and buy that too. A bit of me has Lee in mind for the beret, especially now that Pie has inflicted more damage on his battered trilby, but another part of me worries that giving it to Lee would feel too revealing, like giving away a slice of my heart. What if he didn't like it, didn't want it?

I like Lee Mackintosh. I like him more than any boy I've ever met, and that scares me.

A Christmas tree is delivered on Sunday morning, the tallest, loveliest tree I've ever seen. Sheddie helps to manoeuvre it into the living room, where it is positioned in front of the big bay window.

'Can we decorate it?' I ask Grandma Lou.

'Of course!' she says. 'You make a start . . . I just want to finish the underpainting on my magpie picture, then I'll join you!'

I haul four boxes of decorations out of the attic, and the memories flood back as I unpack an array of lopsided baubles crafted by the two of us in years gone by. My eyes widen as I uncover a cache of neatly découpaged hearts made from kitsch old Christmas cards pasted on to cardboard and sprinkled with glitter – I've never seen them before, I'm certain.

I'm wearing one hung over each ear, like giant earrings, when Grandma Lou comes in with a tray of hot spiced apple juice. 'Ahh . . . Vivi made those, when she was about your age,' she tells me. 'They were her Christmas present to me that year. She was never very keen on art and craft, but she took so much care over these. They're very special to me!'

I remove the hearts from my ears. 'Sorry!' I say. 'How come I've never seen them before?'

'Vivi decided that she hated them, said they embarrassed her,' Grandma Lou explains. 'When the two of you came for Christmas in the past, she would take them down from the tree and pack them away. I think she'd have thrown them in the bin if I'd let her.'

Grandma Lou's eyes mist with tears. 'I can't believe it ever got to this point,' she says with a sigh. 'It grieves me every single day. I've invited Vivi for Christmas, but she hasn't answered yet . . . I'm sure she'll come. She'll want to see you.'

'Maybe,' I say, but I know that neither of us quite believe it.

'She'll come if she can,' Grandma Lou says. 'But everyone here at Greystones is a kind of extended family, really, so Christmas dinner will still be fun. It's always a big, communal affair. D'you remember, Phoenix?'

'Of course I do!'

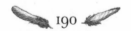

I remember the kitchen full of people cooking, potatoes cooked in cream, nut roasts wrapped in golden pastry and pies filled with veggies in cheese sauce or tahini and tofu, quiches and tagines and bakes – every kind of festive feast except for the turkey. I remember how we used to set up two trestle tables at either end of the long farmhouse dining table, draping them in old sheets tie-dyed green and scarlet for the occasion. The people from the flats, the caravan and the yurt would arrive, each with a dish to contribute, and the celebration would begin.

Christmas Day was a party from start to finish at Grandma Lou's, with laughter, feasting, music, song and chat. I remember suddenly how Willow would plait my hair with ribbons and sing carols to me as Mum sat trying to watch the Queen's Christmas speech on TV. She hated Christmas at Greystones, even then.

Grandma Lou lowers a sixties compilation LP on to the record player, and we set to work. I untangle the fairy lights and put up the old stepladder. It's quite wobbly, and Grandma Lou is still in her green suede hippy clogs, so I climb up to drape the tree with lights and tinsel. Once that's done, we hang baubles from every branch – clumsy handmade ones, classy retro ones, fragile vintage ones and, finally, Mum's découpage hearts in pride of place.

I try to imagine my frosty mother at fourteen years old, cutting out cardboard hearts and sticking on snipped-up Christmas cards and pinches of glitter, but the image won't come. Instead I see a sad-eyed girl looking for love, not so very different from me. Haven't I just forked out most of my pocket money on a garish designer-label scarf because I wanted the heart motif to say the things I can't put into words? Are we really so very different?

Grandma Lou holds the stepladder while I stretch out to fix the star in place at the top of the tree, inhaling that sharp Christmas-tree scent of pine, citrus and nostalgia. We drape the remaining few strings of fairy lights round the window and door and over the big wooden mantelpiece.

'It's wonderful!' she exclaims. 'All it needs is some evergreen branches here and there to finish it off, but I'll cut those next week . . . I want them to stay fresh!'

When we switch off the ceiling light the whole room looks magical.

*

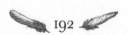

When I come home from school the next day the fairy lights are twinkling as I crunch up the driveway and, inside, the house smells of oranges and cinnamon. I feel the kind of thrill of anticipation I haven't had in years.

'I've been drying orange slices in the oven,' Grandma Lou tells me. 'I thought we could string them together with cinnamon sticks and fir cones to make some Christmas garlands, the way we used to when you were small. I'm making Christmas cake, too!'

I sigh. 'It smells amazing!'

'It does! It's been a funny kind of day – I'm baking to cheer myself up, I think!'

I frown. 'What's happened?'

Grandma Lou smiles sadly, wiping her hands on her apron. 'Sadie from the top flat came over to see me,' she says. 'She and Joe have found a job creating an organic garden in a new shared living community in Spain. They're moving out at the end of the week. I'll really miss her – we went to art college together in the seventies – but this is a wonderful opportunity for them!'

'That's a shame,' I say. 'Who will live in that flat now?'

 193

'No idea. Somebody who needs it, I hope!' Grandma Lou says, dipping a finger into the cake mix and tasting it before adding a glug more brandy. 'I'm a bit late with the cake this year – I usually do it at the end of November because it's better if it has a while to sit – but it'll still be good. And now you're here to help me stir!'

She hands me the big wooden spoon and tells me to make a wish. 'It's a tradition,' she says. 'Go on!'

So I close my eyes and stir, thinking of all the things I could wish for . . . a record deal, a slot on Lola Rockett's New Year show, fame, fortune, no more freckles. Instead, I surprise myself and wish for Mum to come for Christmas . . . which, of course, is the least likely thing of all.

Dear Mum,

I know Grandma Lou has invited you for Christmas already but I thought I would write too because we haven't heard back yet and it wouldn't be the same without you. I know you are very busy but Christmas is a family time, isn't it? I've got your present wrapped up under the tree. I don't know if you'll like it but I hope you will. I helped decorate the tree and also helped to make the Christmas cake. (Maybe I shouldn't have told you that - I don't want to put you off!)

In case you were ____ wondering, my very first performance with the ____ band was amazing. There were tons of people there and we got reviews in loads of the local papers. I have so much to tell you. I hope you can come for Christmas. It's supposed to snow this week, and I know the weather can get wild up in Scotland and I don't want you to get snowed in and miss Christmas completely!

Please come, I really want you to meet my new friends.

Phoenix x

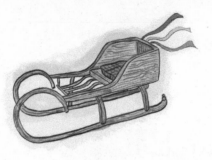

18

Snowfall

On Wednesday afternoon I'm in class working my way through a page of simultaneous equations when it begins to snow. The flakes are big and dramatic, drifting down from a sullen sky like torn paper, falling faster every minute. Everyone has noticed now, and any chance of us finishing our algebra is lost forever.

Kids are at the window, laughing, pressing their noses against the misty glass. Excitement fizzes round the classroom and the teacher doesn't try to fight it because there are only a few days of term left and the chance of getting anyone back to their equations is non-existent.

Dawdling to my last lesson, I stop at an upstairs window to see if the snow is settling, and spot a familiar figure in a shrunken cotton jacket cowering in a doorway round the back of the gym. A telltale plume of smoke rises up through the swirl of snowflakes.

I run downstairs and head towards the gym, my feet crunching through the freshly fallen snow, flakes starring my hair. Sharleen has pushed herself back into the doorway, so she's almost invisible now, but I know she's there and crunch my way over, stepping neatly in beside her so I'm hidden from view too.

'Whatcha want, Posh Girl?' she asks. 'I'm not sharing me ciggies, so you can forget that!'

'I don't smoke,' I remind her. 'Want some chocolate?'

I fish half a bar of Fruit and Nut from my bag and hand it over. 'Haven't you got a proper coat?'

Sharleen shrugs. 'I like this one.'

'Are you still at the B & B?' I ask.

'No, Posh Girl, we've moved into the Hilton. We get room service every night . . . caviar and champagne.' She laughs, a harsh, sad sound that turns into a cough. 'Course we're still there. What did you think, we had a Christmas miracle?'

Words spill out of my mouth before I can properly think them through. 'My gran has a flat going at Greystones. She hasn't advertised it yet . . . Maybe your mum could apply?'

Sharleen rolls her eyes. 'Like we could afford that! Mum's had her benefits stopped. Why d'you think we're in this mess to start with?'

'You could ask,' I persist. 'My gran won't judge, and I know some of the Greystones lot pay their rent with work around the place. Jake's stepdad does . . .'

'Don't want charity. And who'd want to live with a bunch of old hippy weirdos anyway?'

I sigh. 'Fine. I just thought I'd tell you. Gotta go, I'm late for class . . .' I unwind my scarf and shove it at Sharleen, who yells that she doesn't want my cast-offs, that I'm a stupid do-gooder with rotten taste and she wouldn't be seen dead in the thing.

When I look back through the falling snow, though, she's huddled in the scarf and scoffing chocolate. 'Happy Christmas, Posh Girl!' she says.

Back at Greystones, I decide to bake mince pies to take to band practice. I want to show the band how much they mean to me, but in a low-key way, and with Grandma Lou's help I just about avoid burning them to a crisp. I pack them into a basket covered with a checked tea towel, and I feel like Little Red Riding Hood crunching through the snow towards the old railway carriage, although I don't suppose she had a magpie on her shoulder.

I scramble up the steps. Marley and Dylan have got the wood burner going and Lexie has the kettle steaming and everyone is way too excited by the snow to settle. We drink hot chocolate and eat the warm mince pies and Marley tries to enforce a holiday practice timetable that only gives us Christmas Day free, and is voted down in favour of a two-hour rehearsal every other day.

'Where's George?' Romy asks. 'He's really late!'

'Snowed in?' Lee suggests.

'No, he has a Christmas carol concert in town,' Lexie says. 'He told me earlier.'

What?' Marley growls. 'A poxy carol concert comes before the band?'

'I said it'd be fine,' Lexie says. 'It's a one-off, Marley. It's Christmas. Have a heart!'

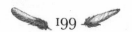

Marley scowls. 'We won't even miss him,' he says, and there's more than a grain of truth in those words. The songs are strong and tight and full of life tonight, even without George's cello pieces. We finish the rehearsal on a high, with lots of hugs and swapping of Christmas cards and speculation about whether school will be open in the morning. When we spill out into the frozen darkness, the snow is falling faster than ever, hiding our footprints from earlier.

There's a brief snowball skirmish with the whole lot of us hopping and slithering about, Pie flying in circles above us, screeching. Soon the snow slides down inside my boots, making my feet wet and cold, and I have snow in my hair and down the back of my neck. I'm shivering, laughing, my cheeks stinging. It's too cold for anyone to want to hang around, and I pull my duffel coat round me and watch my friends slip and slide towards the gates.

I'm about to head for the house when one figure stops and turns back. Lee picks his way back along the drive, stopping in front of me, shivering in his vintage jacket and woolly scarf, snow still clinging to the brim of the battered trilby.

'There was something I wanted to say,' he tells me, and my heart leaps because this time if he asks me out I might seriously think about saying yes. I care about Lee . . . no amount of pretending I don't will change that.

Lee frowns. 'I figured I was probably getting on your nerves, asking you out all the time. So I'm not going to any more. You can't say I didn't try . . .'

He turns away and my heart feels like it's breaking. I've messed up again, let something special slip right through my fingers. Why do I get everything so wrong?

'Lee?' I call out, my voice wobbly with emotion, and he stops, looking back over his shoulder. 'I . . . I was wondering. Do . . . d'you want to go out with me sometime? Just one date, a no-risk, no-strings, trial-offer thing, and if we don't like it . . .'

'Are you serious?' he asks. '*You're* asking *me* out now?'

I shrug. 'Why not? It's the twenty-first century – equal rights for men, women and messed-up kids who wish they'd just said yes the first time you asked . . .'

In the stillness of the softly falling snow, Lee sighs and pushes back the battered trilby. 'Of course I'll go out with you, Phoenix,' he says. 'You know I will!'

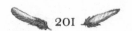

'Not right this minute,' I backtrack. 'It's snowing and I'm freezing and my feet are wet. These boots are soaking . . . and Grandma Lou will have the dinner on . . .'

Lee laughs. 'OK, OK. If this keeps up, the schools might shut tomorrow . . . I could come over? We could go sledging, make snow angels, build an igloo – your wish is my command!'

'All of that!' I tell him. 'Cool!'

His hand traces a path down my cheek, and I shiver. 'Not so much cool as freezing,' he says. 'What happened to your scarf?'

'Lost it,' I say.

Then I grab Lee's scarf and run off through the trees, slipping and sliding across the freshly fallen snow, and by the time he catches me we're both laughing so hard I've forgotten about the cold. Lee pulls me close, his fingers twining into my hair, his breath soft against my cheek. He kisses the end of my nose, and his lips are the only warm thing in the whole of the world.

Next day, the snow is still falling. The world looks like it has been washed clean and dipped in icing sugar, and a

thrill of hope and wonder flutters through me. On a day like this, anything is possible, surely?

I'm up early, stitching magpie feathers on to the charity-shop black beret. I've decided to be brave and give it to Lee after all . . . Perhaps it can say the things I can't quite put into words. My inspiration is the feathered ear cuff Sasha made for me, and I arrange layers of feathers in a fan shape, stitching them carefully so that they stick out a little on one side of the hat. It's not the kind of thing you'd wear every day, but . . . on stage, maybe? I have never seen Lee in a beret, but I know he likes hats and I know he likes feathers, and at the last minute I add a bar of Fruit and Nut chocolate too and carefully wrap it all in tissue paper and hope for the best.

As Grandma Lou and I tuck into porridge, the local radio station announces that all local schools will be closed. An email from Millford Park Academy confirms it, and the whoops of joy and flying snowballs from outside the kitchen window suggest that Jake's family have got the message too. A text from Lee tells me he's on his way.

'There's a sledge in the shed,' Grandma Lou tells me. 'Remember, from when you were little?'

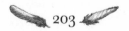

By the time Lee arrives, I'm wearing two pairs of socks, Grandma Lou's gardening wellies, two pairs of leggings, the Bellvale lost-property jumper layered over a T-shirt, and the duffel coat. Grandma Lou loans me a woolly hat and scarf.

'Are you painting again today?' I ask her.

'Yes, while the light's good,' she says. 'And I must get the Christmas greenery in, too . . . I shouldn't have left it so late!'

'Why not ask Sheddie to do it?' I suggest.

'Maybe!'

I pull on my fingerless gloves and crunch along the drive to meet Lee, and five minutes later we're dragging a vintage wooden sledge towards the park. Already the slope is dotted with kids dragging red and blue plastic sledges up to the top and plummeting back down again. We bump into Jake, who is on babysitting duty all day because his mum and Sheddie have driven up to Birmingham with Laurel, Jack and Willow to do their Christmas shopping.

We join forces, trudging up the hill with our sledges before whooshing down again. We keep going until our toes are like blocks of ice and our fingers are numb and Jake's little sisters are tired and hungry.

'Hot chocolates at the Leaping Llama, anyone?' Jake suggests, and the very idea of it sends the two girls into meltdown. 'We need to thaw out, right?'

The pavements are slippery as we drag the sledges back to Greystones. We meet the postman, running late and struggling, what with the Christmas mail and the slushy pavements.

'Want us to take it?' I offer.

'Great – it'd save me going up to the house. Just cards today . . .'

He hands over a bundle of cards and I shove them into my coat pocket for later. Pie dives down from the oak tree to greet us as we leave the sleds inside the gates, hidden behind the snow-topped shubbery, but the snow seems to have put him in a strange mood and he's keen to stay at Greystones, so we head off to the Leaping Llama without him. Well, not everybody wants a magpie in their cafe on a snow-day afternoon.

Hot chocolate revives us all, and then Jake gets a flurry of texts from Sasha and decides to take the girls over to

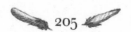

her place for cheese on toast, a Disney DVD and some nail-painting. 'Mum, Sheddie and the others are still in Brum,' he tells me. 'They won't be back for a few hours yet. Were any of those cards for us?'

I pull out the bundle of post and peel off a couple addressed to Jake's family. As I hand them over, I see an envelope addressed to Grandma Lou and me, written in black fountain pen in a small, neat script. My heart twists. Why is Mum sending a card? Why not just bring it when she comes for Christmas? I don't want to know. I stuff the bundle of post back in my pocket and use the long teaspoon to deposit a blob of cream on Lee's nose.

We talk all afternoon. Lee looks at me with bright hazel eyes as if he can see into my soul, and I don't care any more if this ends in tears because right now it feels like heaven. We share a bag of chips and do a snowy tour of Millford, calling in at the garage where Lee's dad works for a mug of tea so strong you could stand your spoon up in it. We go back to the park and make an igloo, then snow angels, then warm up again by taking cover in the park bandstand and making up new dance routines until we're breathless.

206

It's almost five by the time we get back to Greystones. Fresh snow is falling now, and what's already on the ground has frozen to an ice-rink shine, but I'm still wearing Grandma Lou's wellies and I manage to keep the two of us upright.

The minute we step through the gates, I know something is wrong. Pie swoops on me with a piercing '*Crak, crak, craaak!*' and instead of perching on my shoulder he flaps and circles and screeches.

'What's that in his beak?' Lee asks. 'It looks like mistletoe. Weird. Where did he get that from?'

I'm running then, following Pie as he swoops along the driveway and veers off to one side towards the apple trees. As my eyes adjust to the darkness, I spot the stepladder propped up beneath the furthest tree, make out the mound of cut holly branches in the wheelbarrow at its foot.

Beyond the stepladder is the crumpled body of my grandmother. Her eyes are closed, her skin pale as the moon, a sparkle of freshly fallen snow glinting on her brow.

To Louisa and Phoenix,

Merry Christmas
and a
Happy New Year

Best wishes,

Vivi

Unfortunately I shan't make it for Christmas Day, as I have prospective parents arriving on Christmas Eve for a school tour. Driving down overnight would not be advisable. I will do my best to be with you by Boxing Day and head north again the following day. I hope this plan is agreeable to you both. It is unfortunate about Christmas Day but I'm sure you won't miss me in the midst of the usual Greystones festivities.

Vivi

19

Mistletoe

I'm on my knees in the snow, my arms round Grandma Lou, my hot tear-stained cheek pressed against her cold marble one. A terrible fear is unfurling in my gut, a fear that I have lost the only family member who ever really loved and understood me. 'Please, please, please stay with me,' I whisper into her hair.

Behind me, Pie is stalking up and down in the snow, squawking wildly, and Lee is calling 999. I can hear him describing the scene, his voice steady and calm. He drops to his knees beside me and picks up my grandmother's wrist.

'Yes, there's a pulse,' he says into his mobile. 'It's faint, but it's there. She's in her seventies, I think . . . Yes, yes, a fall. She was on a stepladder. Yes, in the snow. No, we don't know how long she's been lying here . . .'

'She's so cold!' I wail. 'So cold!'

I pull off the borrowed scarf and ease it under her head, drape my duffel coat over her. I'm shivering now, my teeth chattering with the cold and the shock. Lee is wriggling out of his jacket, unwinding his own scarf, still on the phone.

'No, no, we won't move her . . . How long will that take? Because she looks really bad, and it's snowing again. Please hurry!'

I tuck Lee's jacket over her legs. One of her clogs is several feet away, beneath the wheelbarrow. 'Why was she wearing clogs to climb a ladder anyway?' I whisper, and then I realize that she gave me her wellies to wear because they wouldn't slip in the snow. This is all my fault. 'Oh God . . . I'm sorry, I'm sorry, I'm sorry! Why didn't I cut the greenery for her? She does everything for me!'

'Hush, Phoenix, it's not your fault,' Lee says.

'Don't leave me,' I whisper against her cold cheek once more. 'I need you. I'm sorry! Please stay!'

Pie screeches again and flies up into the apple tree. A sweep of lights appears at the end of the drive, and

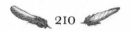

a vehicle bumps along towards us. It's not the ambulance, not yet, but Sheddie's van is a welcome sight. Lee runs up the drive to flag it down and moments later Sheddie and the others are there, and blankets are brought and Willow checks Grandma Lou's pulse again and strokes her hair, and Laurel makes hot sweet tea for the rest of us, and then finally, finally, the ambulance arrives.

I kiss my grandmother's icy cheek, but it's only when the paramedics lift her on to the stretcher and into the ambulance that I see her bony fingers are still clutching a bunch of freshly clipped mistletoe.

If you ever have to go to A&E, try not to go in the middle of a snowstorm, four days before Christmas. It's not a lot of fun. I travel in the ambulance with Grandma Lou, the paramedic telling me not to worry, that she's in good hands, that we did the right thing by trying to warm her up and not moving her.

'There could be broken bones and concussion, but hypothermia is the main concern for now,' he says.

'Hypothermia?'

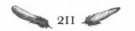

'It's when the body temperature falls to a dangerously low level,' he explains. 'It's especially serious in the very young and the very old, and it can progress quickly. Your gran has lost consciousness and her pulse is very weak . . . We need to warm her up and get her breathing and her heartbeat back on an even keel.'

'I'm scared,' I whisper.

The paramedic squeezes my hand. 'Chin up, my friend,' he says. 'I'm willing to bet your gran is one tough cookie. One of those independent types, am I right?'

'You could say that . . .'

'What was she doing up the ladder in the middle of a snowstorm?'

'I don't think it was snowing at that point, but . . . well, she was cutting mistletoe,' I say, holding up the bunch that I took from her ice-cold fingers.

The paramedic sighs. 'Bless her. If we can get her better, I'll give her a Christmas kiss myself!'

Sheddie and Lee follow behind us in the van, and once Grandma Lou has been triaged and moved to a ward, they sit with me in the waiting area as the doctors prepare to treat her with warm intravenous fluids and humidified

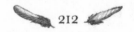

oxygen. Nobody here laughs about getting gran better. Their faces are serious, sad.

'Are you the next of kin?' one nurse asks. 'There are no other relatives?'

Abruptly my brain shifts into gear and I explain that my mum is the next of kin, but that she lives miles away in Scotland and has no idea that anything has happened.

The nurse puts a comforting hand on my shoulder. 'I'd call her, pet. I'd call her right now. She needs to be here.'

I'm in shock, I know. I am colder than the snow, frozen inside, but I know that it's not good when someone tells you that the next of kin needs to be here. It's not good at all. There is no phone signal inside the hospital, so Lee takes me outside and we stand together in the swirling snow as I punch the numbers into my phone.

'Mum? Mum? It's me, Phoenix!' I say. 'Something terrible's happened!'

'Oh, for goodness' sake, what have you done now?' she asks, and tears well in my eyes and spill down my cheeks and I don't even care. 'Phoenix? Tell me!'

'It's nothing I've done,' I whisper. 'Or maybe it is. I should have cut the holly and mistletoe, and I shouldn't

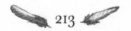

have taken her wellies, and I knew she didn't like the stepladder, but Sheddie was out all day and I didn't know that till later –'

'What are you talking about?' Mum demands, a note of alarm in her voice now. 'What exactly has happened, Phoenix?'

'It's Grandma Lou,' I say. 'She was cutting mistletoe and she was wearing clogs and the stepladder was wobbly, and she must have fallen and we don't know how long she was lying there.'

'What do you mean, you don't know? Where were you, Phoenix?'

'I was out with a friend. We'd been sledging . . . it was a date.'

'It's snowing down there?' Mum says slowly. 'My mother fell off a ladder and lay there in the snow? What are you saying, Phoenix? Is she all right?'

I stifle a sob. 'I don't think so,' I say. 'She's unconscious. Her heartbeat and breathing are very weak. It's hypothermia, I think . . . something like that. The doctors are trying to warm her up, but they said I had to ring you because you're the next of kin, and I know I'm not supposed to call, I know you're really busy, but I think it's serious and I don't know what to do . . . I'm sorry, Mum!'

'Oh my God,' Mum says. 'Of course you had to call! Look – I need to be there. Are you at Millford General? Is anyone with you?'

'Lee's with me,' I say. 'The boy I went sledging with. And Sheddie from Greystones.'

'OK,' Mum says. 'OK. Look, stay there. Wait. I'll be with you as soon as I can. I'm guessing the conditions aren't good where you are, but it's clear up here still so I'll come. It's a long drive, but I'll be as quick as I can, OK?'

'I'm scared, Mum,' I whisper.

'I know,' she says. 'But you have to stay strong for me, Phoenix, you hear? I love you. And just in case I'm not in time . . . will you tell Lou I love her too?'

'Yes . . . yes, sure I will!'

The line goes dead, and I lose any last pretence of holding it together. The tears come again, sad ones and happy ones, tears for Grandma Lou and Mum and me, for three generations who messed things up and hurt each other without meaning to. Maybe it's not too late to fix things?

Lee puts his arms round me and holds me close. My mum is coming, and she loves me. I've waited such a very long time to hear that.

In the end, Lee goes home to get some sleep, and Sheddie stays, the responsible adult in a moth-eaten rainbow-striped jumper and dreadlocks. We sit on the chairs with squashy plastic seats in the private room where Grandma Lou lies, wired up to monitors, drifting somewhere between life and death. Nobody tells us anything, but I'm not stupid – I know we're only allowed to be here because things are serious, because if we go home we might come back at morning visiting time and find we're too late.

Even in the half-light, I can see the drip feeding into my grandmother's hand. Her face, still that awful waxy colour, is half hidden beneath an oxygen mask. A kind nurse gives us blankets and pillows and brings us tea and biscuits. A few hours in, Sheddie wraps a blanket round himself and falls asleep, but there's no way I can. I watch the nurses as they bustle in at regular intervals to change the drip, check the oxygen. I watch the clock as it crawls through the early hours and try not to think of Mum driving down from Scotland through the night, through ice and snow. I stare at the little bunch of mistletoe in my hands and wish I could turn the clock back and do so many things differently.

It's past 6 a.m. when Mum finally arrives, her face grey with worry and exhaustion. Sheddie had woken a few minutes earlier and stepped out to fetch coffee and chocolate, and I have never been happier to see Mum in my life. I step forward, wanting a hug, but this is clearly not an option. We're a messed-up, dysfunctional family, even, it seems, at a time like this.

'I should have known something like this would happen,' Mum says, her face creased with worry. 'Lou is so irresponsible – she always has been! Climbing a ladder on her own in the snow, in those ridiculous clogs! At her age! And you – you were out all afternoon with some boy, Phoenix! For goodness' sake! Trouble follows you wherever you go!'

A flame of anger sparks into life but is extinguished almost at once. What is the point of trying to argue when Grandma Lou is fighting for her life? My shoulders slump.

The kind nurse looks on, her face unreadable, and shame burns my cheeks.

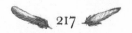

'I'm afraid Louisa is not yet conscious,' she tells Mum gently. 'She's stable, and her heart rate and breathing are steadier now, but we'd really like it if she regained consciousness. She's responding to treatment, and that's good, but progress has been slow, I'm afraid . . .'

'But she will get better?'

'Hypothermia can be a difficult one to call,' the nurse says. 'But, rest assured, we're doing all we can. I'll make sure there's a doctor available to talk to you soon.'

The nurse leaves us alone, and Mum seems to crumble. 'Oh, Phoenix . . . I'm sorry . . . I'm just so wound up, so worried!'

'I know . . . and you're right – it is my fault,' I tell her. 'If I hadn't been out. If I hadn't borrowed her wellies. If I'd cut the greenery for her. I was too wrapped up in myself . . . and I think trouble really does follow me wherever I go!'

'No, Phoenix,' Mum says. 'That's not true – it's me who gets everything wrong. I'm so frightened right now. I was looking for someone to blame, but it's not you – how could it be? None of this is your fault. Oh, Phoenix, she looks so frail!'

I swallow back a sob and move to one side of the bed while Mum approaches the other. I am used to seeing my

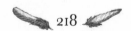

grandmother striding about in velvet tunics with paint-stained fingers and silk scarves in her hair – I forget that she's in her seventies, because she certainly doesn't act like it. I barely recognize this pale, shadow version of my gran.

'I love you,' I whisper softly. 'Please don't leave me!'

Mum wipes a hand across her eyes, blinking back tears, struggling to hold herself together. 'I love you too,' she says, smoothing back Grandma Lou's hair. 'I always have and I always will. I'm sorry if I've hurt you – I know you always did your best for me, did what you thought was right. I'm sorry . . . I'm so, so sorry!'

Mum's head dips down towards Grandma Lou's shoulder, her body shaking with silent sobs that break my heart.

And then my grandmother's eyes flutter open, and the hand without the cannula moves slowly up to hold my mother close.

Sheddie comes in with the coffee, taking in the scene. 'Did I miss something?' he says.

I tie the mistletoe on to the metal bedframe, a talisman for love and luck and hope, and watch the women I love best in the world hold each other tight.

Diary of Phoenix Marlow, age 12

Today my dad cancelled Christmas. I was supposed to be going to stay with him and Weird Wanda in Dubai, and their new baby who looks like a giant uncooked pork sausage dressed in a babygro, but Dad called and said that the timing was all wrong. What does that even mean? Christmas is the same date every year!

Mum said I need to remember that it's quite stressful when you've got a newborn baby, and they probably just can't handle the extra stress of having me around. Extra stress? I'm not that bad, am I?

And I am Dad's child too. I think he is starting to forget that.

Mum said that as a special treat we can go to a hotel in town and have our Christmas dinner there, and then watch a DVD of 'It's a Wonderful Life' back home because it's her favourite Christmas film.

Well, my life isn't wonderful. It sucks.

Also, my new half-brother is called Drake.

I mean . . . . really?

20

Secrets and Lies

Grandma Lou comes home on Christmas Eve in a borrowed wheelchair trimmed with tinsel. It turns out she has sprained her left ankle, but her body temperature, heartbeat and breathing are all back to normal. The paramedic who brought us in actually did track her down and check on her, and even gave her the promised mistletoe kiss.

'That was all my Christmas presents rolled into one,' Grandma Lou says, and Mum rolls her eyes and tells her she's a lost cause.

We settle in for a Greystones Christmas, just a slightly quieter one than usual because the doctor says Grandma

Lou has to rest and take it easy. Clearly the doctor had no idea who she was dealing with, because Grandma Lou is back in her studio that same evening, mixing paint to finish off her painting. Mum and I adjust the easel so she can work from the wheelchair, and then we leave her to it.

I put a Christmas playlist on in the kitchen, and Mum purses her lips but doesn't complain, even though I know she'd rather be listening to something classical. We work side by side, rolling pastry, mixing up the filling for veggie sausage rolls, talking.

'Thank you for coming,' I tell her. 'I was so scared, I thought . . . well, you know. The doctors seemed so worried and Grandma Lou looked so sick, and I thought it was the end, that it was my fault.'

'It wasn't your fault,' she promises. 'My mother is a very stubborn woman – she's been a human whirlwind for years, and she has no intention of slowing down. Perhaps now she'll see sense.'

'You think so?'

'Pigs might fly,' Mum says. 'She's had a scare, though. Maybe she'll cut back on climbing ladders in the snow

while wearing velvet frocks and clogs . . . or maybe not. Who knows?'

'Well, I'm glad you came and I'm glad you stayed,' I say. 'I thought you might go back for those parents who were coming to look round the school . . .'

Mum is silent, and when I glance up I notice that her eyes are damp with tears. 'Of course I came,' she says. 'And of course I stayed. Family comes first – or it should, Phoenix. That's not a lesson I seem to have learned very well, I'm ashamed to say. We're a messed-up family, much as I hate to admit it. The hurt gets passed down to the next in line like some kind of cruel pass-the-parcel game. We take off a layer of wrapping, swallow down some hurt and pass the rest along . . .'

I finish rolling up the veggie sausage rolls and set them neatly on two baking trays for Mum to glaze. 'There!' she says, brushing the flour from her hands. 'One job done!'

Silence falls between us, along with about a million unanswered questions.

'I know I'm not the kind of daughter you wanted,' I say. 'I'm going to try to be better, I promise. Did . . . did you and Dad regret having me? Is that why you split up?'

Mum looks shocked. 'Phoenix . . . what? No! You are totally the right kind of daughter . . . I'm just not very good at being a mother, I'm afraid. I've got so many things wrong. And your dad and I always wanted you – you've no idea how much. We wanted a family and we wanted it to be a happy one, but things fell apart and that was my fault. I had no idea how to be in a partnership, how to give and take. It was my fault the marriage failed, Phoenix, and you were the biggest loser. You wanted to run and climb trees and dig in the dirt, and paint and shout and sing . . .'

'Was that a bad thing?' I ask.

'No! It was – is – a wonderful thing, but I didn't know how to handle it. You were so different from me . . . and you missed your dad so much, of course. I started to get promoted at work – I kept telling myself we needed the money – and, well, running a school seemed a whole lot simpler than being a mum, I suppose. I was trying to do the right thing, Phoenix, I promise!'

The right thing . . . that's all any of us try to do, surely? And yet time after time our best efforts backfire and it turns out we did the wrong thing after all. I'm used to it by now, but I had no idea Mum might feel the same way.

'What about Dad, though?' I ask.

'Your dad loves you, Phoenix,' Mum is saying. 'He's just not good at standing up to Wanda.'

I nod. I think I've known this for a while.

And then Mum is dialling through to FaceTime Dad in Dubai, and after a few brisk words she hands her mobile to me. There's Dad, thousands of miles away, wearing a Santa hat and wrapping presents for Drake and Dara. It's four hours ahead there, almost midnight, but he takes his phone though to the boys' room and I see my little half-brothers sleeping in the glow of the night light, their baby faces flushed with excitement, Christmas stockings hanging at the end of their beds. Wanda leans in towards the screen, waving, wishing me a Merry Christmas.

'I was going to call you tomorrow, Phoenix,' Dad says. 'It's been hectic here – work has been pretty full-on, and the kids keep me busy . . .'

'I'm your kid too, Dad,' I say. 'Even though you're miles and miles away, you're my dad. I need you too!'

He looks startled, then sad. 'I know you do, Phoenix,' he says. 'I'll try to do better. We should set a regular time and day to FaceTime, and perhaps you could come over for a holiday?'

I've heard it all before. 'You always say that,' I challenge him. 'You always promise and it never happens, Dad. How many times have I been to visit you in Dubai? Never. Not once in all the time you've been there. It's never a good time for you, and it never happens. I've never even met my half-brothers. Do you know how that makes me feel, Dad? Do you?'

He opens his mouth to argue, then closes it again. I watch him take a tissue from his pocket and wipe tears from his cheeks, but I'm not sorry I said it. I wish I'd said it years ago.

'Happy Christmas, Dad,' I say, and cut the call.

In the end, it's the best Christmas ever. The fairy lights glitter and Mum doesn't take the home-made heart decorations off the tree, and, even though we decide to skip the mistletoe this year, Lee and I manage a kiss beneath the tinsel-draped chandelier instead.

He loves his feathered beret and gives me a book of photos of an Australian family who have a tame magpie. The pictures are beautiful, but the magpie eventually leaves them and returns to the wild, which makes me sad. 'Pie won't ever do that,' I say. 'He's a hero, now. He saved Grandma Lou!'

'He did, I know . . . but he will go back to the wild one day, Phoenix. He needs his freedom!'

That's something I don't want to think about – not yet.

My other presents include a new iPad from Dad, a pile of books and an emerald-green corduroy minidress from Mum, and a pair of green Doc Marten boots with ribbons instead of laces from Grandma Lou. Everyone comes in from the flats and the outbuildings, and Christmas unfolds around us like magic.

We feast and hug and laugh and play old-fashioned board games, and the adults drink mulled wine and hot port and Grandma Lou DJs, her tinselled wheelchair wedged in beside the record player. The dancing goes on late into the night.

Every day I expect to wake and find that Mum has gone back to Bellvale, but every day she stays. She cooks – no microwave ready-meals in sight – and though she burns the rice and the spaghetti turns to mush and the cheese sauce is more like lumpy mashed potato, she keeps trying. She cleans and lights the wood burner and drags us out for brisk, snowy walks around the park, pushing Grandma Lou in the wheelchair, tucked in under a crochet blanket.

In the evenings she reads us chapters from Dickens' *A Christmas Carol* or asks random general knowledge questions, like a kind of human version of Trivial Pursuit. I see a glimpse of someone I vaguely remember from childhood, a mum who can turn her hand to anything (except cooking), and organize life so it runs like clockwork, making me feel safe. She wears the red silk scarf with the heart pattern every day, even though it clashes with her beige cashmere twinsets and olive-green tweedy coat. Sometimes she links my arm as we walk, and I find myself leaning in towards her.

'Mum,' I say, one day when Grandma Lou is in her studio painting and the two of us are stacking the dishwasher together. 'Remember when you and Grandma Lou fell out, four years ago? We were here for Christmas and something happened and we packed up early and went home ... well, what was it? What made you stay away for all that time?'

A flash of pain crosses her face and her fingers go to the phoenix necklace, tugging and twisting at it. 'Phoenix, come on – that's all in the past. Now isn't really the time ...'

'When is the time, then?' I ask. 'Aren't we trying to be open with each other? I know you've made your peace with Grandma Lou, but what could possibly have been so bad that the two of you didn't speak for four whole years?'

To my surprise, Mum falls apart. My tough, sensible, no-nonsense mother sinks on to a kitchen chair, head in hands, her shoulders shaking, sobbing. I'm not sure I can handle two total breakdowns in the space of a week. I put the kettle on and find the box of tissues.

'Don't cry, Mum!' I tell her. 'It doesn't matter!'

'It does,' she tells me. 'It does, because when your whole life has been built on secrets and lies, sometimes you need to hear the truth. Four years ago, I asked your gran who

my father was. It was a question I'd been asking her ever since I was a little girl, but she'd never tell me. And then, four years ago, she did . . .'

Mum takes a ragged breath in and tries to smile. 'Turns out my father was a man I'd known all my life. When I was little, I thought he was wonderful – I idolized him, followed him about like a shadow . . . but he never belonged to me. He married three times, but never Grandma Lou. They were best friends . . .'

Unease stirs within me. Best friends? Mum was born in 1973, bringing Louisa's ten-year career as a famous model to an end. In that time she hung out with the international jet set. She met Andy Warhol in New York (I wrote about him in art history at Bellvale) and even made the cover of *Time* magazine, photographed on the back of Bob Dylan's motorbike. A famous Canadian songwriter immortalized her in a hit song and legend has it that David Bowie once hid away in the old railway carriage at Greystones, working on an album.

I've heard all the stories, soaked them up with a sense of awe as if listening to a fairy tale or a legend, but I've never heard Grandma Lou describe any of those people as her best friend.

'He never knew, you see, Phoenix,' Mum continues. 'He never knew he was my dad, even though he spent so much time with us. And I didn't know either, but I hoped, sometimes. By the time I reached my teens, he'd lost interest in me. I wasn't this cute little kid who followed him around any more – I was a swotty, introvert, plain-Jane teen who suddenly found my mum's arty, bohemian friends . . . well, silly and childish with their all-night parties and their wrecked careers and their endless stories of fame and fortune.

'One day I was singing to myself, some stupid eighties pop song . . . here in the kitchen, working through a page of fractions homework. He walked in and heard me and laughed, and told me not to give up the day job, and I've never forgiven him for that . . .'

'Who, though?' I push, even though a part of me has already guessed. 'Who told you that, Mum? It was probably just a joke, a throwaway comment. You shouldn't have taken it to heart!'

Mum laughs, but it's a cold, harsh sound. 'Oh, he meant it,' she says. 'I have a terrible voice, I know that now, but when I was your age I hadn't a clue. He knew, though. He would, wouldn't he? He was a pop legend, even then.'

My heart is hammering.

'Four years ago I plucked up the courage to ask Louisa again, because Lord knows I am a grown woman and surely I deserve to know who my own father is. And you know what? She told me. It was him, Phoenix . . . Ked Wilder. Ked Wilder is my father. Your grandfather.'

I open my mouth and close it again. 'B-but . . . I d-don't understand!' I stammer. 'Ked seems so nice! Why didn't he say something? I met him at the gig at the start of December . . . Why didn't he say anything to me?'

Mum gets up, takes two mugs from the cupboard and fishes teabags from the caddy. I can see her putting herself together again, gathering her defences. She pours on the freshly boiled water, squeezes the teabags, adds milk.

'That's just it,' Mum tells me, plonking the mugs down with shaking hands and pushing the biscuit tin across. 'Ked doesn't know. Louisa never told him, and he never guessed. They dated for a while in the late sixties and decided they were better as friends, but when Louisa came back from America, they must have got together again, briefly. It didn't last, and soon after Ked met his first wife – one of those whirlwind romances. They married in a registry office in Camden round about the time that Louisa realized she was pregnant. She kept quiet, let Ked think it was someone she'd met in America. She's kept the pretence up ever since . . .'

'Oh, Mum!' I say.

'That's it, really,' she says. 'Louisa put Ked's happiness ahead of her own, ahead of mine . . . ahead of yours. His marriage didn't last, and he went on to marry twice more. They didn't last, either. Who's to say what would have happened if she'd told him? Didn't he have a right to know? Perhaps I'd have had a father, and they might have found a way to make it work, to stay together. They really do care about each other, I know that . . .'

'It's the saddest thing I've ever heard,' I whisper.

Mum sighs. 'I was angry with Lou for a long time,' she admits. 'I wanted a clean break . . . I passed on her cards and presents, but anything personal, any letters, went straight into the bin. You tried to write too, but . . . I didn't send your letters. I had no right, but . . .'

'You were hurting,' I finish for her. Mum was out of order, but what's the sense in blaming her now? It won't change anything. We're building bridges at last, and that's what really matters.

'Phoenix?' Mum asks. 'Have you seen Louisa's painting?'

I frown. 'No . . . you know what she's like. She won't show anyone until she's finished.'

'I know,' Mum says. 'But helping her these last few days, I couldn't help but see. Come and look . . .'

She pads through the hallway and opens the studio door a fraction, stepping back to let me see.

Grandma Lou sits in front of a huge painting, her back to me, seemingly absorbed in the work of mixing paints on the palette table at her side. The record player spins a Beatles LP, but it's the painting that takes my breath away. The canvas is huge and beautiful, a painting of me and Pie with a young man with blue eyes and a black fedora being towed through an azure sky by a flock of small red phoenix birds. In the distance a woman and child dressed in sari silk are playing with monkeys, laughing, holding hands.

Mum closes the door again, gently, silently.

'What . . . what even is that?' I whisper as she leads me back to the kitchen.

Mum takes a deep breath. 'It's a family portrait . . . the weirdest, most beautiful family portrait I've ever seen. How can I be angry with her, Phoenix? She's lived all this time with the secret . . . and what a bittersweet secret it is!'

'Poor Grandma Lou,' I say. 'Poor Ked!'

'He has no idea that he told his own daughter she couldn't sing, or that the new lead singer of the teen band he's backing is his granddaughter . . .'

I take a deep breath in. 'Mum . . . if you knew how much it hurt for someone to say that, then . . . well, why were you so cold about my singing? You never actually said it outright, but you made it clear you hated it. I grew up believing I had a terrible voice!'

I watch Mum battle with her emotions again. 'I never meant you to feel that way!' she argues. 'I'm sorry if that's how it seemed. I just wanted to protect you . . . I didn't want you in that world, because I'd seen how vain and fickle it could be. And after I'd found out about Ked . . . well, I'm ashamed to admit it, but I hated that I didn't have his talent too!'

'Oh, Mum!'

She smiles sadly. 'I may look like a stuffy old head teacher, Phoenix, but there's still a part of me that never got past the hurt little-girl stage. I told myself I was protecting you from the music world, but perhaps my motives were more selfish than that. I'm sorry, I really am!'

I pull Mum in for a hug and she lets out a deep breath, like she's finally letting go of the worries that she's been holding close for years.

'So . . . Ked and Louisa,' I say, after we pull away from the hug. 'What a mess. Why can't things come out in the open now? Why does it have to stay secret?'

'Lou said there was no way she could tell him . . . He'd be angry, upset, the papers would have a field day with it. She has a list of excuses as long as your arm to explain why he can never know. I don't suppose I'm the type of daughter a sixties pop legend would want, anyhow – I'm too plain, too dull, too ordinary.'

'You're a million miles from ordinary,' I protest. 'You're . . . I don't know, you're a force of nature! You're smart and strong and slightly terrifying. You're cleverer

than anyone I know . . . you run a school, for goodness'
sake!'

Mum laughs. 'Thank you. Only slightly terrifying?'

'OK . . . completely terrifying. But I feel safer with you
than anyone else in the world!'

'That's good to know. There's nothing like a long
midnight drive through a snowstorm to make you think
about what matters in this life. I thought I was heading to
a deathbed, and seriously, Phoenix, I don't think I'd ever
have got over that. I've been given another chance with
Louisa – another chance with you too. I'm not going to
waste those chances. I'm tired of secrets and lies, but I'm
starting to understand why Louisa made the decisions she
did. She was trying to do the right thing. We're pretty
slow learners in this family when it comes to looking after
each other, but whatever else we do, we keep on trying. I
think we'll get there in the end.'

'I wish I'd known all this,' I say. 'I thought . . . well, I
thought you didn't like me very much.'

The words hang in the air between us, heavy and sad,
but they're my truth. It feels good to say them out loud at
last, like squeezing the poison out of a wound and cleaning

it with something stingy to let it heal. I can see Mum fighting to keep back a second wave of tears.

'I love you, Phoenix,' she says quietly. 'I've made so many mistakes, and I'll go on making them, I suspect, but you . . . you are the one absolutely perfect thing in my life, and I am so very proud of you. I love you so much. I'm so sorry if you didn't know that, and – well, I'm just so sorry for everything, really. I'm so proud of you . . . your courage, your spirit, your spark. You teach me more about life every day than books ever could!'

'I love you too, Mum,' I say.

She pulls me close and we cry on each other's shoulders, the kind of messy crying that makes your eyes red and gritty and your nose run and your heart ache, and I wonder why it took so long to work out that no matter how complicated the problem, the answer is almost always 'I love you' and 'I'm sorry'.

I lift up my mug of tea, but the milky liquid spills down my sweater as a piercing yell rings out from Grandma Lou's studio.

'Phoenix! Vivi!' she shouts. 'Come quickly! Ked's on the line . . . you'll never guess!'

Sending by text and will try to get you all on the phone as soon as. BIG NEWS. Like, the BIGGEST. The BEST. Ked Wilder has been on the phone. Someone's had to pull out of Lola Rockett's New Year's Eve TV show with flu and laryngitis. Like, totally lost their voice. She wants us to fill in. US! They're filming it live in London tomorrow night, and they want us in the studio for 6 p.m. I'm ringing round everyone, but please text back and confirm you can be there ASAP. Marley

21

London

I'm up at dawn, too excited to eat, taming my hair with anti-frizz serum and experimenting to see how many 'dress all in black' combos I can come up with. Sasha has been working on the feather design idea and reckons she has enough pieces for the show providing we all turn up in black to give her a blank canvas to work on.

I finally settle on black leggings, black miniskirt, black long-sleeved T-shirt and my new green Docs. We're meeting here at three, a little convoy of cars and van to whisk us down to London, but there's no way I'll be able to settle to anything before that.

I warm up my voice by running through some of the set list as I tidy up the kitchen and wash the breakfast dishes. Mum is taking me and Lee down to the studio, plus Pie, of course . . . no way do I want him to miss out on this. A bunch of VIP tickets have been handed out, so that the families who are driving to London will have seats in the studio audience.

Those left behind will have to make do with the TV.

'Laurel, Jack, Willow and Jake's mum and sisters are going to come up and watch the Lola Rockett show with me,' Grandma Lou says. 'We'll all be cheering you on! Oh, by the way, I meant to tell you . . . there's a new family moving into Sadie's old flat today – Sheddie's helping with the move. A very nice young woman and her two girls. They've had a tough time of it, I think, but hopefully this will be a new start for them. She's going to help me out with cleaning and lighting the wood burner and a little bit of cooking and so on while my leg's healing. Perhaps after that too. I think my stepladder days are over! And hopefully I'll be able to spend more time painting!'

'Oh, that's brilliant!'

'I know, isn't it?' Grandma Lou says. 'In the meantime, could you fetch a few more logs in, so I can keep the wood burner going later?'

I've gathered up an armful of logs from the woodstore, Pie hopping from one shoulder to the other as if supervising, when Sheddie's van pulls up outside the flats. A thin woman with scraped back hair gets out, carrying a suitcase and a couple of bulging bin bags. A teenage girl and a kid bundled up in a too big cotton jacket follow, hauling more rucksacks and bin bags from the van. Something about the scene seems strangely familiar.

'Hey,' I call. 'Welcome to Greystones . . . I hope you'll like it here!'

The girl turns round, one eyebrow raised, unimpressed. It's Sharleen Scott's default expression. 'I'm blaming you,' she says. 'You put the idea in my head. I wish I'd never mentioned it . . . now I'll be stuck living with a bunch of bloomin' hippies! Talk about out of the fryin' pan into the fire. Don't you dare tell anyone at school, OK?'

'I won't!' I say, stifling a grin.

'This is my mum,' she tells me. 'And my little sister, Britney, who is a total pain in the –'

'Pleased to meet you,' I interrupt quickly, grinning from behind my armful of firewood.

'You're Phoenix Marlow, aren't you?' the little girl says, wiping her nose on her sleeve. 'I'm your biggest fan! Can I stroke the magpie?'

Pie preens a little while Britney admires him.

'Not joking, my life is over,' Sharleen huffs. 'Living in a freakin' mansion house with a load of weirdos . . . and a freakin' magpie! You gonna help with this stuff, or not, Posh Girl?'

If there's one thing I've learned about Sharleen Scott, it's that her bark is worse than her bite . . . and that her temper improves hugely when you feed her chocolate. I guess I'll be stocking up on Fruit and Nut, then.

'Who actually is Fliss Benito?' Lee is asking. 'I've never even heard of her!'

'She's the up-and-coming singer who got sick and missed her chance of appearing on *Lola Rockett's New Year Round-Up*,' Marley says. 'The person who gave us our ticket to fame and fortune. Remind me to send her a get-well card in the new year!'

243

'Marley!' I say. 'That's terrible! Imagine how she must be feeling!'

'I don't care,' Marley declares. 'Life's a game of luck, and we just threw a double six. We're going to London!'

I lift up the wicker cat basket with Pie inside it. 'It's quite a long way,' I say. 'D'you think he'll be OK? He doesn't much like travel!'

'We need him,' Marley says. 'Every one of those newspaper pieces mentioned Pie the last time. And Sasha's designed a whole look around him . . .'

'I know, I know,' I say. 'I want him there, but I don't want him to freak out – it'll be noisy and busy and he might not like the lights . . .'

'He'll be fine,' Marley says. 'He'll get used to it . . . you know, life on the road!'

I love Pie, but I don't think I want him to get used to life on the road. Like Lee says, he's a wild creature . . . he doesn't belong in a wicker basket, rattling around from one place to the next. After reading the magpie book Lee got me for Christmas, I'm even more certain that keeping Pie with me, making him tame, may not be fair on him. I

know how important freedom is, after all . . . doesn't Pie deserve that too?

I check my mobile. It's almost three and, though Mum's car and Sheddie's van are parked up and ready to depart, we're still waiting for the others.

'Here's Sasha!' Jake says as a red estate car pulls into the drive. The car is already packed with carefully wrapped costumes and accessories, but there's just enough room for Jake. Bex and Lexie arrive too, their foster parents swooping by to pick up Sami, and Happi's parents call in to join the convoy, although they've already collected Romy. Marley, Dylan and George turn up at the last minute, clambering into Sheddie's van.

Mum emerges from the house, almost glamorous for what may be the first time in her life in a little black beaded dress borrowed from Grandma Lou's extensive collection of vintage items. OK, so she has slung her tweed jacket over the top, but it's still a vast improvement on her usual style. My mother clearly packed and drove to Millford in a mad hurry in the middle of the night, and has now exhausted her selection of horrible cardigans and lurid tweed skirts, which can only be a blessing all round.

'Let's do this!' Sheddie yells. Lee and I jump into Mum's little Citroën, Pie in his wicker basket on the seat between us, and the convoy sets off for London.

RISE AGAIN

I burnt my fingers playing with fire
I stood and stared as the flames jumped higher
My life was like a funeral pyre
Burn it down, burn it down

The smoke got in my eyes and hair
Got into my heart but I don't care
I only just got out of there
Burn it down, burn it down

Ash coated my skin like dust, like dirt
It hid the shame, it hid the hurt
It left a smear on my white school shirt
Burn it down, burn it down

Maybe it's better to live apart
Or maybe I'll melt your frozen heart
Sometimes we all need a new start
Burn it down, burn it down

I was looking for warmth but found a blaze
Was looking for just a little praise
Just looking for you, now and always
Burn it down, burn it down

Choked by smoke I'll run and hide
I'll keep the hurt wrapped up inside
But I'll rise from the ashes with wings spread wide
I'll rise again, rise again

22

Wings

The TV studio is crazy busy. We're assigned a couple of minders and whisked away for an instant soundcheck, because it seems Lola wants to record several tracks for use in future shows as well as have us play live.

'Have you brought the bird?' one of the minders asks. 'The crow? Lola told us to check ... she said it's the perfect gimmick!'

'Pie is not a gimmick,' I argue. 'And he's a magpie, not a crow!'

'I don't care if he's a freakin' flamingo,' the boy says. 'As long as he's here!'

We're dispatched to the nearest dressing room, and Lee opens the wicker cat basket and sets Pie loose. He seems anxious, almost sulky, stalking around the countertops in front of the mirrors – he really doesn't like that cat basket, and I'm not sure he's keen on the whole TV-studio thing either.

Sasha opens her suitcases and boxes and begins hanging up clothes and setting out accessories. There are feathered headpieces and hats, and metallic feathered gauntlets with jagged cuffs that look like armour; there are cloaks and collars and skirts made of net and rags and feathers, and a huge pair of shimmering iridescent wings that glint in the light.

I am mesmerized by the wings. I stare and stroke and press my face against them. 'I made them for you, Phoenix,' Sasha says, lifting my arms and hooking the wings over them. The wings are heavier than they look, held tight by pure magic, gravity and thick black elastic. Instantly I feel different – taller, braver, stronger.

'Oh wow,' Bex says. 'Amazing!'

'Super cool,' Lee says.

Pie perks up and zooms over from the mirrors to sit on my shoulder. '*Crak, crak, craaak!*' he cries.

'Can you move in them?'

I try a couple of dance steps, slowly at first, then faster. Lee plays a raucous trumpet piece and the two of us fall into step together, stomping and strutting and whirling round with Pie hopping easily between the two of us.

'Those wings look incredible,' Marley says. 'Honestly, Sash, they're awesome! How did you find the time to do it all? And how did you find the feathers?'

'The local amateur dramatic society let me root through their wardrobe cupboards,' she says, fitting the feathered ear piece from the Birmingham gig round my ear. 'I found a full-sized blue-green feathered cloak, a whole load of black feather boas and some really cool two-tone fabric. And then I cut and stitched and glued for five weeks solid, because I knew it would look awesome and I knew we'd get our chance sometime . . . I wanted to make sure we were ready.'

'We're ready all right,' Marley says, trying on a cape and gauntlets. 'Oh, man . . . this is our moment, this is our time! Finally!'

The others join him, testing out hats and waistcoats and collars, choosing their stage accessories while Sasha sits me down in a swivel chair to do my make-up. I gaze at my reflection as Sasha sweeps jade-green blusher across my cheeks and paints emerald shadows above my eyes, and I wonder how I can keep up with all the ways my life is changing. Two months ago I believed I was a lost cause, bad to the bone, destined to mess up over and over. My only friend in the world was an adopted magpie, and I thought I had no skills or talents beyond stirring up a bit of trouble now and then to ease the boredom. Since then, I've moved from the Scottish highlands to the English Midlands, joined a band, played my first big gig. I'm falling in love, forging friendships, feeling terrified and thankful, and I'm building bridges with my mum and learning to look beyond her gruff, no-nonsense exterior. I've even helped a girl who bullied me, learned a family secret and made a pact to keep it that way.

Now here I am, with Sasha painting glitter and stars on my cheeks, wearing iridescent blue-black wings and ready to appear on a top-rated national TV show. It doesn't make any sense, but as always Pie is on hand to screech his affection into my ear and remind me not to get too above myself.

Is this what growing up is like?

A make-up artist arrives to help everyone get ready for the show, complimenting Sasha once she sees my make-up and working alongside her to get the rest of the band ready. Lee is wearing his feathered beret, Marley has his cape and gauntlets, the girls have matching net-and-feather skirts and everyone, even George, has either a hat or a headpiece. One of the minders puts their head round the door to warn us that we have five minutes till filming, and then we're back in the studio and Lola Rockett is there, telling us she wants two or three songs to use over the coming months.

'Who did your styling?' she asks, nodding her approval. 'Did Ked get one of his contacts to sort you out? I like it – it's strong!'

'Sasha did it all,' Marley says, and Lola Rockett raises an eyebrow.

'Call me when you're eighteen,' she says to Sasha. 'I can use people like you behind the scenes on the show!'

Sasha looks ready to faint with joy. I wish I felt the same way – terror seems to be the dominant emotion for me right now, but I know that I can ride the waves of fear and survive it. At least, I hope I can . . .

'Counting down!' the cameraman yells, and abruptly I have that top-of-the-hill feeling again, only this time I imagine I'm sledging down, faster and faster, the wind taking my breath, the cold stinging my skin, and I step up to the mic and sing my heart and soul out, and the bright studio lights and the weird, clumsy cameras sliding in and out fade away completely.

I sing four songs in the end, and by the time we finish Lola's eyes have narrowed and her mouth has quirked up into a smile.

'Not bad,' she tells us. 'Not bad at all! I'm glad we managed to squeeze you on to the schedule. I think I'm going to juggle things a little, put you on last – and for two songs rather than one. I want you to do "Fireworks", then we'll do our little chat, our interview . . . and then I want you back on stage for "Rise Again" to take us up to the countdown to midnight. When the clock strikes twelve a storm of gold paper stars will be released from the ceiling, and we'll all sing "Auld Lang Syne" as the credits roll, OK?'

'Whatever you say!' Marley says, eyes wide. 'Thank you! I mean . . . wow!'

'Got that switch?' Lola asks the minders, and they scribble her instructions down on a clipboard. 'The interview segment should be a winner,' Lola ploughs on. 'We're going with the idea of you being schoolkids who've caught the eye of a much-loved pop legend and found yourselves in the spotlight. It's an informal chat with you, me and Ked, to find out the story behind the band. Your head teacher has agreed to say a few words . . .'

'Our head teacher?' I echo. 'You mean Mr Simpson?'

'He's very proud of you,' Lola informs us. 'A big fan, I believe!'

'First I've heard of it,' I mutter, and Marley elbows me in the ribs.

'So, that's the plan,' she says. 'Just a friendly chat, really, and make sure you bring the magpie, of course. Try to forget you're on live TV and kick back and enjoy the party, OK?'

'We will!' Marley promises, but the rest of us exchange panicked glances. This is starting to feel very real, and way more scary than the Birmingham gig.

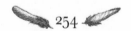

'Hey,' Lee whispers, picking up on my fear. 'Let go and enjoy it. You're a natural, Phoenix. Don't fight it!'

Lola shepherds us through to a crowded room where people in designer suits and sequinned partywear are eating, drinking fizz and laughing together. Are they bands and musicians, or managers, record companies, B-list celebrities? It's hard to tell.

All I know is that Lola Rockett's New Year party – the Green Room version, at any rate – is already in full swing. We're standing on the sidelines, bizarre in our feathers and glitter, me with Pie on my shoulder and shimmering wings of my own. I can see our chauffeurs dotted about the room too – Mum in her borrowed vintage, Sheddie with his dreadlocks and tie-dyed T-shirt, the others looking slightly out of place in Christmas-present jumpers and neatly pressed jeans. It feels like we've gatecrashed some posh showbiz party . . . and actually, we probably have.

I quite like the idea of that.

'Phoenix! Over here!' Ked's booming voice rings out across the crowded Green Room, and my eyes widen because I can see he is talking to Mum.

'Act normal,' she says under her breath as I approach, but there is no normal here, not when I'm wearing feathers in a London TV studio on New Year's Eve and hanging out with an ageing pop legend who doesn't even know he's my grandfather.

'Phoenix, we meet again!' he says. 'You've made quite an impression on everyone – you have real star quality, and I don't say that very often these days. What presence, what energy, what a voice! You must be so proud, Vivi!'

'Always,' Mum says, and I smile, because slowly I'm starting to believe her.

'Vivi has been telling me about your grandmother's fall,' he says. 'We've chatted a few times over Christmas and she didn't mention a thing – a very proud and stubborn woman, our Louisa . . .'

'Runs in the family,' I quip. 'She's fine now, though, honestly!'

'What she needs is a proper rest,' he decides. 'I'll whisk her off to my place in France for a few weeks in the spring – she loves it there! Now, Phoenix, Lola Rockett is over the moon to have you here – it's a huge opportunity, so make it count. Just remember you're at a big party with lots of lovely people, and forget those annoying lights and cameras. Put your heart and soul into it and you won't go far wrong!'

'I'll try!' I promise.

Ked is whisked away to be mic'd up, and Mum breathes a sigh of relief. 'I haven't seen him in decades, but he hasn't changed,' she tells me. 'He's a force of nature, and he likes things to be done his way!'

'That runs in the family too,' I point out, and Mum has the grace to laugh.

There's one last band briefing with Lola Rockett, now transformed into her TV persona in a slinky silver dress and a fancy hairdo so stiff with lacquer that it doesn't move at all. We meet the other musicians who will be performing – five acts in all, and each of us with a story. There are identical twin girls singing Americana folk, a grime collective from east London (one of whom happens to be a junior doctor), three students who met on a gap year in Australia and a grandmother from Cardiff who sings a cappella with the voice of an angel. I think briefly of Fliss Benito, who should have had our spot on the show, ill with laryngitis, and wonder if she's sitting up in bed in some faraway town, dabbing at tears, ready to watch her hopes and dreams wash away.

Life – it's a snakes and ladders game.

'You're here because you're different, you're new and you have a great backstory,' Lola declares. 'Our viewers are going to love you, I know it!'

We are ushered into the main studio at last. The place is decorated with stars and vintage wall clocks and set out like a hipster venue, with retro sofas and mismatched tables and chairs all bunched round a small stage. There are lights and cameras everywhere, and the audience are already in place. I spot Mr Simpson sitting primly at one of the tables trying to make conversation with Mum, Sheddie and a pink-haired woman in a polka-dot dress. I vaguely remember her from Grandma Lou's bonfire party, and Lee tells me in a whisper that she's the librarian from the library the band helped to save in the summer.

We are seated on sofas and armchairs in an alcove lit with fairy lights, and Lola Rockett steps up on to the stage to get the party started.

New Year's Resolutions of Phoenix Marlow, age 14

Turn over a new leaf (I know, I know, another one)
Stay out of trouble at school
Help Grandma Lou more around the house
Write more songs, practise singing every day
Keep in touch with Dad (he's useless, so I'll have
to do it)
Learn to accept that a messed-up family can still be
very cool
Believe in myself

23

Lola Rockett's New Year Party

By the time the cameras begin to roll, we're drunk on thrills, terror and pink lemonade, which the waiters are handing out in champagne glasses. We watch the first couple of bands perform and see how Lola Rockett interviews them between the sets, spinning their stories into TV magic.

There's a knot in my stomach, a frisson of fear. Turns out it all feels very different when you know your mother and your head teacher are in the audience, and that's without even thinking about the people watching at home. Will my old Bellvale classmates see me? Will they laugh? By the time the minders come to take us on stage, nausea

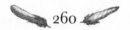

tilts the room a little and I'm actually frightened. This isn't so much freewheeling down a hill, nor even sledging – it's more like jumping out of a plane without a parachute, but a part of me loves this feeling.

The cameras home in on Lola Rockett in her silver dress, giving us a hyped-up introduction, Pie chirrups softly into my ear and Lee steps up beside me and squeezes my hand.

'Wing it,' he whispers, and I realize just in time that I have wings and won't need a parachute after all. I have Pie and Lee and Bex and the others – I am not alone. I look into the audience and spot Sheddie and the other parents; my eyes lock with Mum's, and I can feel her love and pride.

I step up to the mic and jump into the song.

I'm so lost in the music by the time we finish that the roar of applause washes over me as we run down from the stage to join Lola Rockett on the sofas. Ked is sitting on one of the armchairs now, as well as Mr Simpson and the pink-haired librarian.

'I think it's safe to say we're ending the show – and the year – on a real high,' Lola Rockett says as we settle ourselves down. 'Let's meet the Lost & Found . . . a high-school band with a magpie mascot and a very cool backstory! Lexie, Marley, you started the band, is that right?'

'We did,' Marley says smoothly. 'Funny really . . . the Lost & Found was never meant to be a band at all, it just kind of happened by accident because I'd misunderstood the poster, but it was clearly meant to be!'

'Absolutely!' Lola agrees. 'Lexie, tell us about the band's name.'

Lexie grins. 'You could say that we were all a bit lost before the band got going, and that we found each other,' she says, and the rest of us nod our agreement. 'There's a lot of talent in the band, but also a lot of love and friendship. We look out for each other, we support each other, and we try to help others if we can, too –'

'For example, Sami, a young Syrian refugee who made the terrifying journey from Syria to the UK before joining the band!' Lola Rockett cuts in. 'Is there anything you want to tell us about that, Sami?'

Sami blanches visibly, shaking his head, and Lola tells the camera that he's feeling a little emotional and moves

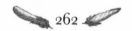

right along. 'Helping others is also how the band met Miss Walker from Millford Library, isn't that right?' she says. 'The Lost & Found used to practise there, didn't they?'

'Yes, until the council announced they were closing it!' Miss Walker responds. 'The Lost & Found decided to put on a festival to save the libraries, and guess what? The council changed their minds!'

Lola Rockett is nodding. 'And of course that's how the band met the legendary Ked Wilder. Ked – you headlined the festival. When did you realize that the Lost & Found were hot property?'

Ked tilts his black fedora hat back and leans in to the camera, smiling. 'It was pretty much straight away,' he explains. 'I've been in the music business a long time, and I know raw talent when I see it. Talent alone isn't always enough, but, as you can all see, the Lost & Found have something more . . . that perfect mix of charm, style, determination and passion. They came down to my recording studios in Devon in the October half-term, and I can promise you that they have a very bright future ahead of them!'

Lola explains to the camera that the band have recently had a change of line-up, and the camera zooms in on me as I'm asked to stand up and give a little twirl to show my wings.

'Phoenix, watching you wow our studio audience tonight, it's hard to believe you only joined the band not long ago,' Lola says. 'The songs you're performing tonight are both songs you've written – have you always wanted to be a singer-songwriter?'

'I think it's in my blood,' I reply, trying hard not to look at Ked. 'I've always loved singing, and I've been writing lyrics for as long as I can remember. I'm not the only songwriter in the band, though – Lexie is brilliant, and neither of us could do what we do without Marley's help. The Lost & Found is a real team!'

'Tell us about the magpie!' Lola exclaims. 'Not every band has such unpredictable backing vocals!'

I reach up to stroke Pie, smiling. 'I rescued Pie when he was tiny. Someone had shot his mother with an air rifle, and he wasn't big enough to look after himself, so I put him in a box and fed him cat food. He got tame really quickly, and when I joined the band he started coming to practices. He's quite musical, I think!'

'What's fascinating about the Lost & Found is that all of you attend the same small secondary school in Millford ... I'd like to ask your head teacher what he thinks of it all! Mr Simpson, what is it about Millford Park Academy that has made it the perfect place for all this talent to grow?'

Mr Simpson beams. 'We're a very nurturing school, of course,' he boasts. 'It's no accident that these teenagers have discovered and developed their skills under our expert guidance ... we've helped and supported them every step of the way. I'll definitely be buying their first record!'

He smirks at the camera while I battle hard not stick my fingers down my throat. I mean, seriously ... hypocrite, much?

Our minders appear just out of shot, a warning that we'll be back on stage any minute.

'That brings me to my final question,' Lola is saying. 'The Lost & Found are a new band, not yet signed to a record label and with no CDs released as yet. Are there any plans for that to change? Ked, do you have any news for us?'

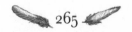

Ked grins. 'It's funny you should ask that, Lola, because I do have a little surprise for the band . . . I've been in talks with a major record label. It just so happens that Josh Okabi from Wrecked Records has been able to join us here tonight . . .'

The camera swings round to focus on a hipster bloke in a three-piece suit and *Peaky Blinders* cap. 'Welcome, Josh!' Lola Rockett simpers. 'So Wrecked Records have some news for us all?'

'We do,' Josh says. 'I'm pleased to announce we have a record deal for the Lost & Found . . . and we're very much hoping these amazing kids will sign in the New Year, with a single and a tour to follow!'

A record deal? A single? My eyes open wide, my mind whirling, struggling to take it in. A glance at my friends shows wide-eyed joy on some faces and blank horror on others . . . Sami and George seem especially stunned. Lee reaches across and squeezes my hand as we run on to the stage while Lola Rockett winds up the interview. 'The Lost & Found are definitely my top tip for stardom in the coming year . . . don't forget you saw them here first! Here they are one more time, playing us right up to midnight with another original song, "Rise Again"!'

This time, I don't have to talk myself up – I'm already buzzing. Studio time, a CD, a record deal . . . my heart is racing. Lee's trumpet solo begins and I fall into step beside him, the two of us mirroring each other's steps, owning the stage. And then I'm singing, soaring, Pie on my shoulder as we sing towards the New Year.

It's all so perfectly timed . . . the last chord dies away and the applause begins, and Lola Rockett runs on to the stage.

'This is it,' she cries. 'Time to say goodbye to the old year and welcome in the new! I hope you've learned well and I hope you're ready for what lies ahead! C'mon, count with me . . . ten, nine, eight, seven, six . . .'

The audience join in and we're all counting together, and as the clock strikes midnight a net of tiny gold paper stars is released, and they float down around us like stardust.

Phoenix
(Ked Wilder, 1969)

She was like wildfire
The wind in her hair and the stars in her eyes
I always dreamed I'd fall in love with trouble.

She walked through fire to be with me
She lit the blaze and helped me see
But she was made of smoke and flame
Impossible to tame.
She was like wildfire
The wind in her hair and the stars in her eyes
It's not easy when you fall in love with trouble.

Sometimes the smoke got in my eyes
Sometimes the truth looked just like lies
She wanted the world to see her shine
But she was never mine.
She was like wildfire
The wind in her hair and the stars in her eyes
It's lonely when you fall in love with trouble.

I tried to cage her wildfire ways
I tried to fight the burning blaze
I wasn't strong enough to stay
And so I walked away.
She was like wildfire
The wind in her hair and the stars in her eyes
I was a fool to walk away from trouble.

She lost her spark, the fire burned low
She told me that she loved me so
And from the ashes she rose once more
A phoenix – stronger than before.
She was like wildfire
The wind in her hair and the stars in her eyes
I let her go and all that's left is trouble.

24

Afterwards

Afterwards a lot of things happen. We hug and kiss and wish each other Happy New Year and try to take in the bombshell news about our new record deal. I can't even begin to process it. The party goes on after the cameras switch off. Mr Simpson is dancing with Mum, which makes me feel queasy, but so many people are coming up to us and saying how thrilled they are about the record deal that I focus on that instead. Marley chats for a while with Josh Okabi, his smile so wide I think his face might crack.

And then we're back on the road, whizzing north, checking phones jammed with New Year greetings from friends and family and messages on social media from people we've never even heard of. When we drove to London, the band's Instagram page had roughly three thousand followers. By the time we're approaching Millford again, the number is closer to twenty thousand and rising. Maths is not a subject I usually struggle with, but I cannot get my head around this.

'Not bad, Posh Girl,' Sharleen's message says.

Lee is asleep on my shoulder, our hands entwined and resting on Pie's basket.

'Ked asked me where I got my phoenix necklace,' Mum says into the silence. 'I told him Louisa gave it to me on my sixteenth birthday, and he went very quiet after that. Do you think . . . that perhaps he gave it to Louisa in the first place?'

'Very possibly,' I say. 'Perhaps . . . could he be putting the pieces together?'

'I don't know,' Mum says with a sigh. 'He asked me if I liked his song "Phoenix". It's one of his best-loved songs. You loved it as a child . . .'

I still love it, of course. I've always loved it, the song that seemed to be about me, the song that taught me that

a fiery nature was nothing to be ashamed of. It's the first song that snagged my imagination, hooked me into the idea of writing. I have a printout of the lyrics folded up inside the Quality Street tin.

'I told him I knew it well,' Mum continues. 'Lou used to sing it to me when I was little, as a lullaby. I wanted to be the girl in the song . . . the wind in her hair, the stars in her eyes. Obviously, that wasn't me at all, but when you were born I wanted that magic for you.'

'Oh, Mum!'

'It all looks a little different to me now,' she goes on. 'I think the song's about Louisa – it got to number one the year after they first split. He gave her the necklace, he wrote the song for her . . . he knows, Phoenix. He's guessed, I'm sure of it.'

I sigh. 'Well, maybe it's about time he did.'

'Maybe it is,' Mum says, and we drive on into the night.

Back at Greystones, Grandma Lou has fallen asleep on one of the velvet sofas, a crochet blanket tucked round her, and the next day her eyes mist up as she tells me how much she loved the TV show. Lee comes over and shows us the Twitter feed and catch-up link for the show, with comment after comment from people who loved the Lost & Found.

The local press turn out in force, all keen to point out that they've supported us from the start. Marley and I do a radio interview with a cheesy local DJ called Barney Bright, and the local BBC news programme films a piece in the old railway carriage, asking us how we feel now that a record deal is all but signed and sealed.

Mr Simpson takes Mum for a coffee at the Leaping Llama on the pretext of asking if she thinks a new musical-theatre group might be a good idea for Millford Park Academy. I almost puke at the idea of him drinking coffee with my mum (she promises it's not an actual date) but she has to drive back to Scotland to get ready for the new term at Bellvale, so disaster is averted. For now.

Saying goodbye is hard. Mum is brisk and no-nonsense right up to the very last minute, and then her fierce, ice-maiden mask slips and I realize that it has been an act all along, this frosty facade.

'I've tried to be strong for you,' she says. 'I've tried my best, but all I've managed to do is hurt you. I'm going to

do things differently from now on, Phoenix. I'm not saying I'll get everything right – I won't – but I want you to know I'm trying. I love you and I'm so very proud of you. I always have been and I always will be.'

She holds me close and I cry all over her red silk scarf, and then she gets into the car and drives away, and I stand at the gates waving until she turns the corner and disappears from sight.

Ked emails to suggest we travel down to London in the February half-term to meet Josh and the others at Wrecked Records and map out a plan for our first single and tour. 'This is life-changing,' he tells us. 'It's a done deal, but I want you all to be very clear about what's involved. Take some time to think about it.'

Marley calls a meeting at the old railway carriage to discuss the email. The day is frosty and the wood burner is roaring. Dylan drums out a backbeat while Lee and I make mugs of hot chocolate and wait for the others to arrive.

'They're late,' Marley grumbles, breaking open the Jaffa Cakes. 'Today of all days!'

It's another five minutes before the others arrive, all together and looking gloomy enough to make me anxious. Something's wrong, I know it is.

'Better late than never,' Marley says sourly. 'What kept you?'

'We went to the Leaping Llama,' George says calmly. 'We wanted to talk about stuff.'

'That's why we're here,' Marley says. 'And if you wanted to discuss band business, why didn't you invite the rest of us?'

'They invited me,' Lee says quietly. 'I said no.'

'I didn't get an invite!' I say. 'I don't get it . . . what's going on?'

'Things are changing – well, they've been changing for a little while now,' Lexie says, but she doesn't look happy. 'We wanted to talk it through . . .'

'Without the rest of us,' Marley snaps.

'Without kicking off World War Three,' Bex replies. 'C'mon, Marley, we've got big stuff on the horizon. Some of us wanted the chance to discuss it away from band HQ, that's all.'

Marley scowls. 'Great,' he says. 'We've just had the very best news ever. We have a big-label record deal . . .

next we'll be recording our first single and planning our first UK tour! Didn't I tell you it would happen?'

'Only about a million times,' George says.

'Yeah, well that's called faith and determination, George, you should try it sometime,' Marley snaps. 'So, who wants to tell me why this sent you all scurrying off to the Leaping Llama for a secret meeting? Is this some kind of mutiny, or what? Are you going to set me adrift in an open boat and steer the band on without me?'

'What are you talking about?' I say, alarmed now.

George shrugs. 'Look – the band's changed, lately,' he says. 'The style is different since Phoenix joined. No offence, Phoenix, it's not your fault – it's how things are working out, that's all. I don't have much of a part to play now, and to be totally honest . . . well . . . I don't think I belong in this band any more.'

'You do!' I argue. 'Of course you do! You can't go now . . . not when we're so close to making it! If you feel you're not a big enough part of it, then we'll put some extra cello melodies in, right, Marley?'

Marley is stony-faced. I think he'd rather smash George's cello right over his head.

'Phoenix, listen,' Bex says. 'This isn't just about George. It's like Marley says . . . the record deal changes everything. It's going to turn our lives upside down, and not everybody wants that . . .'

Marley throws his half-empty hot chocolate mug against the wall, where it smashes into pieces, leaving an explosion of brown liquid to drip down on to the floorboards. Pie squawks in alarm, and Happi, ever the peacemaker, jumps up and gets a cloth to clean it up.

'Not everyone wants us to succeed?' Marley roars. 'Seriously? Was this no more than a game to you? All those rehearsals, all those gigs, a week working with Ked in Devon, endless press coverage, a TV show . . . and suddenly you don't want it any more? Give me strength!'

I take a deep breath. I've seen Marley angry before, but never like this. Lexie puts an arm round his shoulder. He doesn't shake her off, but his fists are clenched and his jaw is tight, as if he's battling to keep a lid on things.

'That's not what I said at all,' Bex says gently. 'Of course we want the band to succeed – we all want that. It's just . . . well, we're moving on to a new chapter. It's amazing – awesome, really. And it's been your dream for so long . . .'

'But not yours?' Marley counters. 'What are you saying, Bex? You're dropping out too?'

Bex looks exasperated. 'Look, Marley, I have GCSEs coming up this summer . . .'

'So what?' Marley scoffs. 'I do too. Who cares?'

'I care,' Bex points out. 'Those grades matter to me – but I've given it a lot of thought and talked it through with the others, and I'm staying, if you'll have me. I don't want to pass up this opportunity. And someone needs to be there to call you out when you go all tyrant on us . . .'

Marley's shoulders slump with relief. 'Don't scare me like that, Bex! I thought this was some kind of mass exodus for a minute . . .'

I start to laugh, but nobody else is smiling and as I tail off into silence Lee sits down beside me, sliding an arm round my waist. Lexie's eyes are a little too bright, as if she's going to cry. Happi is chewing her perfectly painted fingernails, Jake is staring at his shoes, and Sami is trying to hide behind a fall of bird's-nest hair.

'Thing is, Marley, not everybody came to the same conclusion,' Bex says.

'I'm going to step down,' Jake says into the silence. 'I've loved every minute of the Lost & Found, but you don't need me now, and Sash feels the same. We'd both love to work in the industry some day, but the record company are going to want professionals to do the sound and the styling now . . .'

'Sorry,' Sasha adds. 'We'll always support you, always . . .'

Marley nods. 'I get that,' he says. 'It makes me sad, but yeah, I get it.'

'I'm out too, Marley,' Happi says. 'My parents are never going to agree to a UK tour and missing school. They're pretty strict, pretty old-school, you know that, and, if I'm honest, a pop career is not what I want either. I'm sorry. Maybe if this chance had come later on . . .'

Marley hangs his head. 'But you're brilliant, Happi!' he says. 'I knew it'd be a tough call getting it past your parents, but . . . can't you talk to them again?'

'I will leave also,' Sami cuts in. 'I'm sorry – you are my friends, my lifeline. But I have missed so much school the

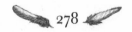

last few years . . . I do not want to miss more. I want to stay here, with my mum and my sister and my aunt and uncle. I will work hard and get the grades for art college. You will be fine without me.'

'Sami, mate, no way,' Marley says, and I'm not the only one who can hear the tremor in his voice. Lee holds me closer, hardly daring to breathe. Bex and Romy shift in their seats, looking guilty, because of course they must know what's coming.

'Marley, you must have known we couldn't go on forever,' Lexie says softly. 'You're so talented and so full of ambition and big dreams, and I'm glad they're going to come true . . . you deserve them to, all of you deserve that . . .'

'Lexie, don't,' he croaks, but she shakes her head gently and puts a finger against his lips.

'I've loved the Lost & Found,' Lexie tells him. 'I really have, but it is changing . . . and that's a good thing, Phoenix, before you say anything! It's *your* songs Lola Rockett wanted on her show, *your* fierce, feisty style. You don't need me any more. I love playing with words and imagery – it's fun, but I'm not really a musician. I never

have been and I never will be . . . It's time for me to step back, Marley, OK?'

'It's not OK, no,' Marley says. 'It's really, really not!' He's on his feet, pushing Lexie away, stumbling past the drum kit, shoving his way to the back of the old railway carriage, wiping his eyes on a sleeve. 'Get out, will you? Please, all of you. You don't have to be here any more, OK? Give me some space. Get out!'

I open my mouth to speak, and find that for once I have no words.

Marley drags open the door of the little compartment at the end of the carriage, the space Jake's mum uses for aromatherapy and reflexology appointments.

'Just go!' Then the door slams behind him, and Lexie stands uncertainly, Sami at her side. George, Jake, Sasha and Happi get to their feet too.

'Really sorry,' Lexie says. 'It was never going to be easy, but . . . well, we wish you all the best, you know that, right?'

'We know,' Lee says. 'We know.'

And, just like that, half of the Lost & Found walk away forever.

FLY AWAY

I knew you from the beginning,
You were battered and broken and lost.
I knew you would fight and be winning,
Come through, no matter the cost.

Chorus: Spread your wings and fly now,
Spread your wings and soar.
Leave the hurt behind you,
Freedom matters more.
One day I'll fly away with you.
One day I'll fly away.

They told me you would steal from me,
My treasure, my silver, my gold.
You stayed with me, you helped me see,
Love cannot be bought or be sold.

Chorus

They say wild things cannot be tamed,
That you'll leave me alone one day,
If you leave, you won't be blamed
But please don't leave me, stay.

Chorus

You taught me how to live my life,
To be strong and wild and free,
To leave the trouble and the strife
And learn to be true to me.

Chorus

25

Picking Up the Pieces

The band survives, of course. We pick up the pieces and move forward, practising every day. We've lost our backing singers, our flute and cello and one of our violins – and lost our first and perhaps our best songwriter . . . but we still have each other.

After all, we are the ones who really need the Lost & Found. We can't give it up no matter what. Marley is music mad, obviously, and crazy ambitious. Dylan doesn't care about anything but playing the drums. Lee has found a place where he can dance and play and act the idiot in a feathered beret, far away from grease, grime and car engines. Bex needs the band to blot out a troubled childhood, and I'm not so very different – for both of us it's a chance to spread our wings and soar. For Romy the Lost & Found is an escape from looking after her mum, who's chronically ill. A cousin moved down from Scotland at the start of January to take over as carer, and Romy is blossoming before our very eyes.

We have drums and bass and lead guitar, a trumpet for drama, a violin to tug at the heartstrings. We have determination.

'We even have a magpie,' Marley adds, but I've been thinking a lot about that just lately. The first faint stirrings of spring are here, and Pie no longer waits for me each afternoon in the old oak tree. He's often missing in action for days at a time, probably off in the park, flirting with the girl magpies, ruffling a few feathers.

He has always been happy enough at rehearsals, but I know deep down that he didn't enjoy the big Birmingham gig, that the TV studio made him anxious and fretful. He hates the cat basket, and taking him to London – or, worse, taking him on tour – would not be fair. 'He's a wild creature,' Mum had said last year, and finally I am beginning to understand that.

If you love someone, set them free . . . isn't that what they say?

'I think Pie's got a girlfriend,' I tell Marley. 'He's stepping back from the public eye for a while, to focus on his personal life.'

'Please tell me you're joking,' Marley says.

'Sadly not,' I say. 'He'll still be a staunch supporter . . . available for occasional photo shoots and railway carriage band practices and one-off local gigs, but he doesn't want to go on the road. Sorry.'

'Never trust a magpie,' he says with a sigh.

So I stop calling Pie, stop looking for him, let him go.

It leaves a hole in my heart that might never heal, but still, I know it's the right thing to do. Pie has always been much more than a magpie. He's taught me how to love, how to care, how to be brave, how to find my voice. He's taught me how to rise from the ashes.

A phoenix is a magical creature, a bird from the world of myths and legends, of fantasy and dreams. You're never going to spot one in the wild – or even in a zoo or a conservation centre – but that doesn't mean they don't exist. Maybe it's just that we make the mistake of looking for plumage the colour of fire and flames, when any magical creature worth knowing would take care to disguise himself ... maybe in white and blue-black feathers with a sheen of oil-slick green?

I place a gleaming tail feather in the Quality Street tin, smiling.

As for the band dropouts, Marley gets over his disappointment and bridges are built. We keep on sitting at the big corner table in the school canteen, because we were never just band mates but also friends, the kind of friends who can weather a storm or two.

'We always had too many people for a band,' Lexie points out. 'The record companies will probably prefer the new slimmed-down version of the Lost & Found!'

And that's exactly what happens. We go to London at half-term and meet the record company, and they tell us they love us and will move heaven and earth to make us famous. They want more songs like 'Fireworks' and 'Rise Again', and it doesn't seem to matter about not having a cello or a flute. They ask about Pie though, and, while sympathetic about his new romance, suggest he joins us for publicity shoots now and then. 'He's a unique selling point,' they insist.

'No, he's a magpie,' I reply. 'A wild creature with the freedom to live however he wants to, OK?' They have to settle for that.

Wrecked Records put us into Ked's recording studio in Devon to make an EP – three tracks, with 'Rise Again' to be released as a single. We miss three weeks of school, but Ked arranges a tutor to make sure we stay on top of schoolwork; it's especially important for Bex with GCSEs looming. While the EP is being mixed and mastered, we do a ton of publicity. Wrecked Records have sent out a press release proclaiming that we are the next big thing, tipped by Lola Rockett and Ked Wilder to turn the current music scene on its head.

We are interviewed by national newspapers and Sunday magazines, websites and teen blogs and a whole raft of kids' magazines, and I manage to enlist Pie to appear in most of them. The magazines cast Marley as the cool, ambitious power behind the band, Dylan as the cute and enigmatic drummer, Lee as the energetic, eccentric joker.

Bex is the smart and slightly scary punk kid and Romy is the girl-next-door type with a penchant for fifties frocks and bows in the hair. Me? I'm the flame-haired firebrand with the magpie mascot, fierce, feminist, the face of the band.

A picture of me in the blue-black wings with Pie on my shoulder appears on the cover of a music magazine with the tagline 'Forever Phoenix' and Lola Rockett promises to devote a whole programme to the issue of whether the Lost & Found can rise from the ashes of a stale and worn-out music industry and usher in a new era of originality, talent and raw energy. TV cameras track our discussions with Wrecked Records and our days in the studio, and plan to follow our progress as the proposed tour zigzags across the country.

Our first single, 'Rise Again', is released on 1st June in a blaze of publicity and begins climbing the charts. It's like the world has already decided we're something special.

Wrecked Records have agreed to hold back the tour until Marley and Bex's last exams are over, so we set off the day after they finish, with a tour bus and driver provided by the record company, on a whistle-stop tour of the UK.

'You'll never guess,' Bex tells us. 'Matt Brennan got caught cheating in his English Lit. exam – he had a whole bunch of Shakespeare quotes written on his shirt cuffs! He's been disqualified, obviously, and Mr Simpson says he's been expelled too. That won't look too good on his application for a journalism degree, will it?'

'Who said there was no justice in this world?' Marley crows, and I smile. Matt, who lied about Sasha and the band to the tabloids and then tried to con me into dishing more dirt on them, will learn the hard way that cheating never pays.

So the tour begins, and it's a bit like setting out on a school trip without any teachers on board. Ked is keeping a steady eye on our business interests, but the record company give us a young tour manager called Mike who tries and fails to keep us in check. He's like a supply teacher who can't quite keep the class from ripping the school to bits, and there's lots of squabbling, backchat and bad behaviour. Lee does cartwheels and handsprings up and down the aisle of the bus, and

Moody Mike puts on his sunglasses and pretends to sleep through it all.

We plot our journey from London to Brighton, Norwich to York, then on to Edinburgh, Glasgow, Liverpool and Cardiff and home at last to Millford. Mum comes to the Edinburgh gig with four of my ex-teachers from Bellvale, and they stand right at the front, cheering and yelling after every song and splash out on Lost & Found T-shirts from the merch stand.

The venues range from cute old-timey theatres to modern leisure centres, but wherever we go there are hordes of pre-teen kids. The girls scream and swoon for Lee, Marley and Dylan but they absolutely idolize me, Bex and Romy, begging for autographs and selfies afterwards. 'I want to be just like you, Phoenix,' ten-year-old girls tell me after every gig. 'You're my hero!'

It's surreal. Wherever we go the papers report on our success, and every show sells out.

The tour takes a fortnight, with a few days off for rest, and we are to end up back in Millford in time to headline their summer festival. Last year, Grandma Lou and the Lost & Found cooked up the festival between them to help

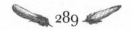

289

save Millford's threatened libraries. Now the festival looks set to be an annual event – and we're top of the bill.

We travel from Cardiff to Millford, but we set off later than planned and the timing is tight. By the time the tour bus ditches us at the park, the festival is in full swing. Moody Mike delivers us to the stage to soundcheck, then shepherds us through to the Green Room. I've seen a lot of Green Rooms since joining the band – this one is a big marquee, and when we step inside, tired from two weeks on the road, a roar of cheers erupts.

'Wow,' Bex says into my ear. 'Look at that!' A giant banner – WELCOME HOME, LOST & FOUND – is hung along one side of the tent, and a crowd of friends and family are waiting to greet us. I know I'm not the only one to melt inside at the welcome.

Grandma Lou, elegant in teal-blue velvet, her red hair piled up and bound with a blue silk scarf, takes my hands. 'Phoenix, I've missed you so much,' she tells me. 'Just look at you, following your dreams! We're all so very, very proud of you!'

I look over Grandma Lou's shoulder and there's Mum, looking slightly less stern and much more colourful than

usual, a purple cashmere cardi over her Lost & Found T-shirt and a mustard and mauve pleated skirt. My heart is so full it might actually burst . . . I only saw her a few days ago in Edinburgh, yet she's rushed down to surprise me here as well. I'd run right into her arms, but Millford Park Academy's head teacher is standing right beside her, an arm hooked through hers, smug and smarmy in a brown-checked wool suit.

'You know Stanley, don't you?' Mum says. 'Mr Simpson to you, of course!'

'Your mother bought me a T-shirt, too!' he tells me, lifting his suit jacket aside to reveal the offending item.

Nightmare. Seriously. In *so* many ways. It's great to see Mum happy . . . but, boy, does she have rotten taste in men.

I see Ked, our mentor and manager, the man who may or may not know he's a jigsaw piece in our mad, mixed-up family. He is rakish as ever in his black fedora hat, telling Marley that the record company have reported a huge spike in sales this week. Our first single has now reached number three in the charts, and Ked seems to think we'll hit the top spot next week.

On Marley's other side is the cute waiter from the Leaping Llama, an arm draped lazily round Marley's shoulders, in full flirt mode.

Ked steps up beside me, grinning. 'I couldn't resist popping up to see your show, Phoenix,' he says. 'I'm so proud of you. I've been spending a lot of time lately with Louisa, talking about the past, putting things together – things I should have worked out long, long ago. We have some catching up to do, it seems, you and me and Vivi. Louisa and I got a lot of things wrong, but it's never too late to start putting them right, is it?'

'No . . . never!' I tell him, wide eyed.

Grandma Lou is glowing as she looks on, and I don't think it's just the suntan from her stay in Ked's villa in the south of France. Ked's hand is wrapped round hers, best friends and long-ago lovers, ageing rabble-rousers, a messed-up family tied together by secrets and love. I can't help smiling. I don't think I'd change a single thing about any of them, and a whole new chapter looks like it's about to begin.

Of course, family isn't just the people you're related to – it's all the people you love. Lee, Marley, Dylan, Bex and Romy are family now, too, partners in crime and creating havoc, the people who listen when I'm sad and missing home, who understand what it's like to spend six hours straight in the studio and then do it all again the next day, and the day after, and the day after. They understand the sick feeling you get before a gig and the soaring joy when you're up there in the spotlight. They know me better than I know myself.

That's what the others gave up, I guess, along with the long hours and the pressure, the roller-coaster highs and lows. Lexie, Sami, Jake, Sasha, George and Happi are here too, all of us together again. There's laughter and hugs and talk, and then Moody Mike looms up, telling us it's time to go.

As we file out of the Green Room, we run into a family coming in. The man is tanned and anxious-looking with horn-rimmed specs and thinning hair, the woman beside him tired and cross, wearing too much make-up, an unflattering dress and high heels that are sinking into the grass and giving her a slightly lopsided appearance. She grips two bemused flaxen-haired toddlers by the hand.

'Phoenix!' the man says, and my heart stills. I'd know that anguished wail anywhere.

'Dad . . . Wanda . . . what are you doing here?'

'We're in the UK so we can catch up with my folks,' Wanda begins, but Dad interrupts.

'No, Wanda, we're here to see Phoenix,' he says firmly. 'We've been following your progress, love, and when Vivi told us about this gig I knew we had to come over. We wouldn't have missed it for the world! I'm so very proud of you, Phoenix! We'll be out there, cheering you on!'

'Aww, Dad . . .' I don't get the chance to say any more, because he hauls me in for a hug and whispers in my ear that he's sorry, that he swears things will be different from now on. I don't know whether to believe him, but, let's face it, I've turned over enough new leaves of my own not to at least give him another chance.

Released from the hug, I lean down to say hello to Drake and Dara, the two half-brothers I've never even met until now. They look a little overwhelmed, but also very cute and possibly cheeky. Dad and Wanda may not be as perfect as I'd like them to be, but there is still time to train Drake and Dara, surely? I'm pretty sure I could be the best-ever bad influence and big half-sister.

'Phoenix, what's the big hold-up?' Moody Mike yells, and I'm whisked away, promising to catch up with Dad after the gig.

Moments later, we're standing in the wings gathering our breath and trying to focus as Pretty Street, the hip-hop band who supported us in Birmingham before Christmas, wind up their set and run offstage. I recognize their friendly backing singer and dancer, Bobbi-Jo, but I can't quite believe my eyes when Sharleen Scott, dressed in a lycra minidress, follows her offstage.

'Break a leg, Posh Girl,' she says, and I laugh, because when we first met Sharleen's swift kick to the shin almost did just that, and now here she is, somehow part of a band after all, dancing rather than singing, wishing me luck.

Maybe the last set of a two-week tour is always the best, or maybe it's because we're home at last, or because we know there's so much love out there in the crowd, but the gig is electric from the very start. We're on a high, feeding off the audience buzz, digging down to find energy where we thought none was left and spinning it into gold. I can see Dad and Wanda in the crowd, each with one of my half-brothers on their shoulders, arms waving ... it's seriously weird.

The set flies past, and then it's the encore, and Marley steps up to the mic and announces that some very special guests will join us to play the last two songs. George runs on with his cello, Sami with his flute and Happi with her violin. Even Lexie, Jake and Sasha are here with tambourines and smiles on their faces, and when Ked joins me at the mic, the crowd go crazy.

'Ready, kiddo?' he asks.

'You betcha, Gramps,' I tease, and although he leans in to hug me, laughing, I am willing to bet not a single soul in the audience of thousands watching us has a clue what they've just witnessed.

We launch into a cover of 'Phoenix' in honour of Ked, and the crowd go wild. They don't hear him tell me he'll have to add an extra verse now, to give the song a happy ending, but they definitely see the huge smile that puts on my face. The very last song is 'Rise Again', and as I start to sing the whole world seems to shift before my eyes, jagged and bright and broken and beautiful, as if all the feelings, good and bad, are too close to the surface to be hidden any more.

I'm on the last chorus of 'Rise Again' when I look up at the darkening summer sky and see a black-and-white bird swooping low, circling above the crowd, gliding in soundlessly to land on my shoulder. Lee has to take my hand because tears are streaming down my cheeks, and there's an explosion of camera flashes and the TV camera rigged up in front of the stage zooms in to capture it all.

Friends are forever, even the magpie kind.

Dad, Weird Wanda and the cheeky half-brothers have long since retreated to the safety of their hotel, with promises to do better at keeping in touch, but, even after they've gone, the Green Room party lasts late into the night.

The moon is high in a star-bright sky by the time we head back to Greystones, a big crowd of us – Grandma Lou, Ked, Mum, Mr Simpson, Jake and his family, Sharleen and hers, and assorted others, to carry on the fun. A distant glimpse through the big sash windows reveals Grandma Lou's family painting, now hanging in pride of place on the far wall, no longer a secret.

Lee and I linger for a while by the wrought-iron gates, saying goodnight . . . and then it's past midnight so we say good morning too. I kiss Lee's nose and tell him that I love him, laughing as the tips of his ears go scarlet and knowing I'll never get tired of seeing that. At last Lee heads off to his own house, his own family.

I walk up the long gravel drive alone, and I can't help remembering that chilly day when I pitched up from Bellvale with a wicker cat basket and a thick layer of dust and ashes stifling my soul. So much has changed since then.

The Lost & Found are on the edge of something awesome – fame and fortune and a possible number-one hit – but, no matter how successful we get, I don't think I will ever be happier than I am right now. I have the coolest boyfriend in the world, the best friends, a magpie pal who thinks he's a phoenix and the maddest, loveliest, most messed-up family ever . . . who knew?

Anything is possible if you spread your wings and fly.